All the Grains of Sand in the Sky

Eugene Miller and John Reinke

All the Grains of Sand in the Sky

The story, all names, characters, and incidents portrayed in this production are fictitious. No identification with places, buildings, and products is intended or should be inferred.

For information about special discounts for bulk purchases or to book an event with our author(s), please contact EFM Management at www.efm-management.com.

Hardcover ISBN: 979-8-218-94409-4
Paperback ISBN: 979-8-218-94407-0
Ebook ISBN: 979-8-218-94408-7

Book Cover by Ganna G.

First Edition

Chapter One

As I sat in the airport, I couldn't help but notice the atmosphere was much quieter than usual. It was California, so I was used to people running late for their flights or arguing with the gate agents about their bags not fitting in the little metal box. The Oakland airport had smaller TSA lines, much smaller than those at the San Francisco or Los Angeles airports. Even so, I was able to get to the airport an hour before my flight and still had plenty of time to buy snacks and find a seat away from the people who showed up.

As I passed through the security line, I locked eyes with the Hudson News store, instantly craving something sweet. I pulled my luggage behind me as I entered the market and headed straight toward the beverage cooler. I grabbed an oversized and overpriced bottle of water before walking toward the candy aisle.

Scanning through the options, I couldn't settle on what I wanted. Chocolate sounded good, but so did something gummy. Sour never failed, but salty didn't either. I stood there, examining the aisle for a good five minutes before someone approached me. "Finding everything alright, hun?" a lady's voice asked from behind.

I turned around, seeing an employee smiling at me, and said, "Yes. Just trying to make sure I make the right choice!"

I proceeded to reach for a bag of Skittles, which were my favorite candy for long flights. After grabbing the bag of Skittles, I walked up to the register and was greeted by the same lady.

"That'll be $12," she said, smiling as if she hadn't just given me the most ridiculous price in the world.

"Oh, wow." Surprised, I pulled out my credit card and tapped it on the reader.

"Yeah, cost of things nowadays is crazy," she said. "Economy's really something, huh?"

"Yeah, it is," I responded.

"Have a nice flight," she said while handing over my receipt.

I walked out of the store and toward the flight monitor. I scanned each departure time on the screen until I locked onto flight 5683 en route to Taveuni, Fiji. I walked toward my gate; it was on the other side of the concourse. People were crowding the walkway, lining up to board far earlier than they were supposed to.

As I neared my gate, I saw an open row of seats on the far end of the seating area. I walked in that direction but noticed they were reserved for handicapped flyers. I looked at the row next to it, and there were two open seats. I had to pick between sitting next to an elderly lady with a walker blocking the seat or next to a charming young man.

I opted for option two, as not only did I not want to ask the lady to move her walker, but I found the man to be quite attractive. Generally, I wasn't this confident, but something in me said otherwise. Maybe it was the kindness of the lady working the cash register. Maybe it was the job opportunity I was taking across the world. Whatever it was, I was feeling it.

"Excuse me, is this seat open?" I asked.

The man looked up at me and said, "Only if you're not going to sit here."

"Oh…" I paused for a moment, trying to make sense of what he had said to me. Oftentimes, I was the friend that would take an extra minute to understand a joke or sarcasm, and that was the case now.

"I'm joking," he said. "Sit down." The man was on his tablet, looking at what appeared to be baseball statistics.

We both laughed, and I took a seat since there were almost twenty-five more minutes until we could board.

"Oh, ha. Funny…" I said. "Thank you." From my pocket, I suddenly felt my phone buzz. It was an email from my new boss, Victor Evans. Victor was the Superintendent at a small school in Taveuni, and he asked me to teach English for the summer at the recommendation of one of my favorite college professors. I pulled the phone out of my pocket, eager to see what the message said. The email read:

SUBJECT: Welcome to the Garden Island!

Dear Noah Ellison,

We are thrilled to be welcoming you to Taveuni, Fiji! You've impressed many of your fellow cohorts with your academics, and we all look forward to meeting you. I will be waiting for you at the landing strip when you arrive this afternoon. My other teachers can't wait to work with you!

See you soon,
Victor Evans
Taveuni Learning Academy
Superintendent

I began to feel nervous the more I thought about how boarding was about to begin. This was going to be the longest flight I had ever been on. I had never done great with motion sickness, so I could only imagine how this flight was going to be. Before this, the longest flight I had taken was for seven hours from New York City to London, and I got sicker than a dog after that. The flight to Fiji was roughly eleven hours—eleven hours I likely won't soon forget.

I looked over once again at the man who allowed me to sit next to him; he was tan, toned, and handsome. He had curly, dark brown hair and perfect skin, the kind of looks that a model might have. It had been quite a while since I'd put myself out there, but something about him made me feel more confident. His presence was intimidating, and part of me wondered why I didn't just find an open seat at a gate or two away. But I was here already, and leaving now would be far too embarrassing. I leaned over toward him and said, "Hey, sorry about before. I'm Noah. Isn't this exciting—flying to Fiji? Have you ever been on a flight like this before?"

"Of course," smirking and chuckling to himself before continuing, "So many."

I smiled back. "Really? This will be the longest flight I've ever been on alone."

"Yep. That's crazy," he said with another small chuckle. "Flights can be so long."

"I'm so nervous. I've never been this far away from home, not to mention the fact I'll be on a plane alone! I hope I don't get sick… or lost!" I said, wondering if he would find that weird. *Was I starting to ramble?* I felt like I'd make a fool of myself if I did.

"What are you going to Fiji for?" he asked, thankfully ignoring my comment about getting sick.

Being confident, I straightened my posture and replied, "I'll be teaching English this summer at a small school on the island."

"See, you have something to look forward to. No need to feel nervous," he replied.

This made me feel good knowing that he was probably right.

"What made you want to teach in Fiji?" he asked.

"I just finished my Masters in English at UC Berkeley, and I was invited to teach abroad before coming home to find a full-time job."

"So, you're smart?" he asked.

"I don't think so," I said sheepishly. "I'm just dedicated to my craft."

We both laughed.

A female voice came over the loud speaker, telling us it was time to begin lining up to board. Everyone around us simultaneously stood up, grabbed their things, and crowded toward the walkways so they didn't have to be at the end of the line.

"What's your name?" I asked, as we stood up and collected our things from the floor around us.

"Marcus," he said. "Good luck with your thing. Maybe I'll see you on the plane."

"Don't worry about it," I replied, not wanting to seem desperate. I'd hoped that maybe talking to him would ease my nerves. "Bye!" I couldn't help but feel slightly rejected by his disinterest in my conversation.

As I stood next to him, I couldn't help but let my eyes wander around his body. He was so tall and had such a muscular body. He had a noticeably large bulge in the front of his pants, and when he took strides, I noticed his very plump rear end—something that had always been attractive to me.

I noticed he had an earbud in his left ear, so I wondered if he had actually paid attention to most of what I told him. I brushed off my feelings of rejection and found a spot in line. I thought he would get in line next to me since we were sitting together, but he made his way to the very end of the line, probably trying to fly under the radar. I wondered to myself why he was taking a trip to Fiji; he'd never told me that. I wasn't sure I wanted to know. He didn’t seem like someone I’d be friends with in an ordinary situation, let alone being together on an island for an extended period of time. He seemed cool—the type of cool that didn't participate in high school band.

The line moved quickly, and I was becoming more anxious by the minute. I found my boarding pass, presented it to the gate agent, and walked down the jet bridge; I was one step closer to being in Fiji.

Chapter Two

After walking halfway down the aisle, I found my seat; one row behind first class. A window seat with plenty of legroom. I watched as everyone boarded the plane—still no sign of Marcus. In the process of boarding, we'd split up. Our enticing half-conversation left drifting in my mind.

After a few more minutes of scanning each passenger that had stepped onto the aircraft, I saw Marcus. He looked around, and I was wondering if maybe he was trying to find me, too. As he started looking for his seat, he walked down the aisle and locked eyes with me. We smiled at each other as he continued walking toward the back of the plane.

I turned my head and saw he sat in a seat a few rows behind me. The seat next to me was empty, but I wasn't sure whether someone was running late for their flight or if the seat was unsold.

I wished Marcus had taken the seat next to me, since we talked at the airport—knowing my neighbor would have probably helped me get through this long flight. I looked out the window and saw everyone's bags being loaded onto the plane. I saw a plane take off in the distance and realized that would be me in just a short time.

I heard the boarding door close, and the flight attendants began their safety briefing. Being as nervous as I was, I paid extra attention when they gave a demonstration on how to use the life vest under the seat. I've watched far too many movies where flights end in chaos and panic to not pay attention now. I was practically an expert in things going wrong.

When the demonstration finished, I turned around and saw Marcus staring down at his phone. He was running his hands through his hair, his loose curls spilled over his forehead. He didn't seem anxious about flying. He didn't seem to think we might crash. That must have been nice.

As we prepared for takeoff, the plane began drifting backward, and the cabin lights dimmed. I watched the runway slowly as we came to a stop for a few moments and the ground crew retreated back toward the jet bridge. I saw the light-up orange sticks being waved around, and the people holding them looked like ants on the ground below. The plane started moving forward, and we were getting ready to take off. As we neared the runway, I looked over at Marcus, and we made eye contact once more. I tried to play it cool and pretend like I was looking around the plane and not directly at him.

I took my earbuds out of my carry-on and put them in my ears as the plane turned onto the runway. I sorted through my playlist and settled on listening to "So Long, London." We sped up, and the plane lifted off the ground. My ears popped as we started going through the clouds. I took a few sips of water, in a last-ditch attempt to calm the anxiety.

After a few minutes, the cities and buildings on the ground faded away into a gray blur of puffy clouds. The sun was so bright that I had to lower my window shade a bit. A few minutes into the flight, a ding sounded over the announcement system, and I knew that meant it was time to begin in-flight service. I had spent years learning about commercial planes and what many of the chimes and tones meant. I thought about going to flight school instead of being a teacher.

"Hello!" The flight attendant, a young woman who appeared tired and restless, asked, "What are we drinking?"

"Just a can of Coke, if you have it!" I replied.

"Would you like a shot of rum in that?" she asked with a laugh.

"I don't think I should this early in the day… I'm fine, thank you," I answered.

"Alcohol in the air doesn't count," she chuckled while handing me a chilled can along with a bag of sea salt potato chips before moving on to the next passenger.

— — — — — — — —

After several hours in the air and many episodes of *Abbott Elementary*, I'd finished my Coke and made it through half of my oversized bottle of water, so I needed to use the bathroom. I stood up, spotted the closest bathroom, which happened to be right behind the man on the flight, and walked that way.

As I walked toward him and the bathroom, Marcus waved at me and took one of his earbuds out of his ear. That surprised me, I didn't think he wanted to talk to me anymore.

"Sorry I couldn't hear you in the airport. I was listening to a podcast," he said.

"No worries," I replied. "I was just rambling."

"You still feeling nervous?" he asked.

"I'm doing better now, but I think I drank too much water." I laughed, "I really have to go to the bathroom."

He chuckled as we smiled at each other, and I took that as my cue to continue walking toward the bathroom. I'd forgotten how small airplane aisles were, which made shuffling around a bit more complex than it needed to be. But after squeezing through several passengers moving seats and a couple carryons that were definitely not supposed to be out on the floor, I finally made it to my destination.

After finishing up in the bathroom, I returned to my seat and sat down, looking out the window as I noticed we were now flying high over the ocean. I started becoming anxious again when I thought about how high up in the air we were. Sometimes, the best thing to lower my anxiety was a little rest. We had maybe seven hours left in the sky, so I wanted to finish up my drink and snacks before preparing to take a much needed nap. I reclined in my seat, put the hood of my hoodie over my head, and closed my eyes.

— — — — — — — —

When I woke up, we had about an hour left before we would land. I sat up and saw Marcus sleeping in his seat a few rows back. Too bad the seat next to him was occupied, because I would have had no problem sitting next to him and continuing our conversation from earlier. I returned my seat to its upright position and thought about what to do for the rest of the flight.

"Flight attendants, prepare for landing," a deep male voice said over the intercom system. Suddenly, I heard the double-chime, which meant the plane had been cleared to land. I couldn't have been more excited.

The cabin lights illuminated, and the crew swept through the cabin collecting everyone's trash. I started to feel nauseous, lightheaded, and I started gripping onto the armrests on my seat as the plane descended from the sky.

The island looked absolutely breathtaking. The trees, the sand, the water, all of it looked like something out of a luxury vacation brochure. The village I'd been assigned to was settled at the base of a breathtaking mountain, like nothing I'd seen before. I'd only ever seen pictures of Fiji online, so seeing it in person made the moment seem almost unreal.

Chapter Three

The small landing strip below looked like it had been carved straight out of a jungle. From my seat, I could see the dense green pressing in against all sides, only a narrow stretch of concrete holding it back. The plane's wheels hit the ground harder than I had expected, and the sudden jolt sent my stomach into a slow, uneasy roll. By the time we slowed to a crawl and taxied toward the small terminal, I knew I was in trouble.

The air inside the cabin felt thicker when we finally came to a stop. Everyone stood, stretching and reaching for bags, but I stayed in my seat, gripping the armrest and forcing myself to breathe through my mouth. Marcus was a few rows ahead, his backpack already slung over one shoulder, not even glancing back. I couldn't decide if I envied his calm or resented it. I was too busy waiting for my ears to pop. *Did he see me sitting here? Is he going to check in on me?*

I thought the plane was hot, but stepping off the plane was like walking into the boiler room of hell. The humidity clung instantly, wrapping itself around me and my woven white sweater and corduroy pants. I felt sweat beginning to seep from my skin. My stomach lurched, and I barely made it a few steps off the tarmac before my potato chips and Coke started shouting for a way out. The sour taste burned my throat as everything I had tried to keep down finally gave up the fight. My knees wobbled, and I braced a hand against my thigh, wishing I could vanish into the ground before anyone noticed.

Of course, people noticed. A couple of passengers hurried past, trying not to look like they saw me, but I could feel the sting of curious eyes all the same. The air smelled of jet fuel and damp vegetation, and the mix did nothing to help me recover. All I wanted was some fresh air. It stank; it was hot; and now I was sick. I wiped at my mouth with the back of my hand and tried to stand up, attempting to keep myself at least a little bit composed. The bag on my shoulders made it harder to return to a somewhat normal posture, but I made my best effort to do so.

I was still bent forward, swallowing down the lingering taste in my mouth, when I heard a low chuckle behind me. Marcus had stopped a few feet away, hands stuffed into his pockets like he was watching something mildly entertaining. "Rough landing?" he asked. "Man, if a little turbulence knocks you out, I can't wait to see how you handle island life!"

Heat rushed to my face, and not from the sun. I straightened slowly, wiping my palm across my shirt to get rid of the sweat sticking to it. "I'm fine," I muttered, though my voice came out thinner than I'd meant. "Just a little motion sickness." He looked back at me and grinned like he'd scored a point, then continued to saunter off toward the terminal without another word.

Before I could think of a decent comeback, a large hand landed on my shoulder. The stranger gave it a firm squeeze, the kind that was meant to steady me, though it also reminded me I had someone watching. "You alright?" His tone was brisk, businesslike, as he leaned in slightly. I looked up and noticed it was Victor, my new boss. He looked middle-aged, maybe five foot four, with wispy gray hair. I didn't expect him to be as short as he was. I had only ever seen him over Zoom calls or at his tiny profile picture on Google.

"Don't pay too much attention to Marcus. You shouldn't be seeing him too much. He's a missionary," he said. "He'll be making rounds through the village all day while you're at the school." Victor patted my back in an attempt to make me feel better, clearly not realizing the news he'd just shared twisted my stomach even tighter. A few burps rose up, and with each one, I feared I would vomit once more.

His words made me freeze. I couldn't do anything except blink. I turned to face him fully, sure I must have misheard. My stomach twisted again, but for a different reason this time. "He's the missionary?!" The words slipped out louder than I intended, drawing a few curious stares from the trickle of other passengers heading inside.

Victor raised his eyebrows at my reaction, then nodded toward Marcus, who was already pushing open the glass door to the terminal. The word "terminal" seemed to only mean a small room here in Fiji, nothing like the Los Angeles airport where there were multiple terminals, each with at least forty gates. Here there was one runway, one terminal, and just enough space for one plane. "Last-minute choice," he explained. "The church we work with couldn't find anyone else willing to take on the assignment. Nobody wanted to commit to a year out here, so when they saw someone finally apply, they gave it to him. I'm not even totally sure he has all the credentials, but, they say he's passionate, and that's half of what it takes right there!"

I stared at Victor, trying to process that the guy who spent the entire flight with his headphones in, the guy who had just made fun of me for throwing up on the tarmac, was supposed to be the spiritual guide for this island.

He must have caught the doubt on my face, because he added, "Don't worry, it's only a trial week for him. We'll see how he does before anything's final." He straightened his tie, though it was already perfectly in place, then gestured for me to follow him toward the terminal. "The pastor said if things go south, they'll just send a church intern to take his place."

The words *trial week* stuck with me, heavy and unsettling, as I trailed behind him, still trying to imagine Marcus in the role he'd just been assigned. I forced out a laugh that didn't sound convincing even to me. "Well, I won't hold my breath," I told him, though the words came out sharper than I'd intended. He didn't respond, just gave a tight nod before moving on with the group toward the terminal.

Dragging my feet a little, I grabbed my single duffel bag from the luggage cart outside. It was light enough—about a week's worth of clothes, a few toiletries, and the leatherbound journal my mom had insisted I pack. She told me to pack a few condoms, "in case I meet a lucky man," but I rolled my eyes and told her this was strictly a work trip. Definitely not everything I wanted to bring along, but everything I could fit in a duffel bag meant for a year. Seeing the others roll massive suitcases beside me made my bag look almost laughable, like I hadn't gotten the memo we were allowed to pack more. Still, I swung it over my shoulder, trying to remind myself that traveling light was practical, even if it also made me feel unprepared.

The walk from the airstrip into the village was shorter than I expected. The path was worn and dusty, cutting through lush green that rose taller the farther we went. The air smelled faintly of earth after rain. It was heavy and sweet, my glasses fogging up the further we walked. I used my one clean sleeve to wipe the lenses in a halfhearted attempt to clean them and continued on with the group.

Eventually, we came to a row of small, thatched bures lined up along one edge of the village, their palm-leaf roofs sloping low and their wooden doors set in uneven frames. The bures looked like something straight out of a vacation brochure. A budget vacation. They looked simple, almost fragile, but there was something inviting about them, like they had been here longer than any of us would be. They certainly looked it.

Victor stopped walking beside me and pointed toward the third bure in the row. "Let me see here…" He said, examining his clipboard. "You are in Bure Three. I think your roommate is already there," he said, "I've got to run, but make yourself at home!" he added, already moving on to direct the others. My stomach tightened as I stood there in the sand staring at it, key clutched in my sweaty palm. I already had a fear of meeting new people, and the thought of stepping inside and meeting whoever I'd be living with for the next year made me feel almost as queasy as the plane ride had.

The closer I got to the door, the slower I let my steps become. The bure's walls were made of bamboo, with some accents done with what looked like woven reeds. Through the small gaps I could hear muffled sounds—shuffling, grunting, and the scrape of something against wood. My pulse quickened. From the porch, I shifted my duffel from one shoulder to the other, trying to buy myself another second before the inevitable moment.

After what felt like forever, I finally slid the key into the lock. The metal clicked loudly, and for a moment, I thought about backing away, pretending I had the wrong place. Or maybe even begging Victor to pull some strings and get me my own place all together. But it was too late now to turn back. As long as I had my own space, my own room to clear my thoughts, I'd be fine. Finally, I began to push the door open when I was met with my new roommate in the entryway.

My new roommate was tanned, tall, broad-shouldered, and unmistakable. Marcus. He stood just a few feet away, his own bag tossed carelessly on the floor beside him. His eyes widened when he saw me, and for a long beat of time, neither of us moved an inch.

We stood there for a few moments frozen in place, staring at each other, the silence stretching out until it felt unbearable. I could practically hear my own heartbeat hammering in my ears. I mustered up all my courage and finally broke the silence.

"You've got to be kidding me," I said. "We're going to be rooming together?"

"Welcome home," Marcus said.

Chapter Four

"Hey, Teachy," Marcus said. He leaned casually against the doorframe, arms crossed, like he'd been waiting for the moment I came home just to deliver that line. "Surprised to see you again so soon."

"You're telling me…" I muttered, shifting my duffel bag up higher on my shoulder. "Good to see you again, Marcus…" My voice sounded flat even to my own ears, but I couldn't do much about it. The situation already felt surreal, but out of all the people I could be forced to share a bure with, why did it have to be him? The guy I could barely tolerate on the flight, the guy who laughed at me when I puked on the tarmac, the guy who drove me insane with his level of self righteousness, I couldn't stand him! And now here he was standing in front of what was going to be my home for the next year.

Trying to focus on something other than the knot of tension forming in my chest, I cleared my throat. “So… where’s my room? The bure didn’t look that big from the outside. At least tell me I’ve got a bedroom with a window.” I was hoping there was some trick to it, maybe a back hallway or a hidden partition that gave us each our own hideaway. Somewhere, anywhere I could escape to when I didn’t feel like being around Marcus. Which would probably end up being all the time.

“Lemme stop you right there…” Marcus raised an eyebrow and smirked. He looked down on me with that stupid confidence he loved to carry, clearly knowing something I didn’t. He didn’t move right away, letting the silence drag long enough to make me more uncomfortable than I already was. “You had one thing right about the place. It’s not that big,” he finally said, his tone maddeningly calm. Then he pushed off the doorframe, stepping aside so I could see inside.

I could feel my face drop the instant Marcus backed away. The interior of the bure was nearly barren, stripped down to only the essentials. The essentials for a walk-in closet, maybe. There were no halls, no rooms, just the bure. The woven walls let in small slivers of sunlight, and the air smelled faintly of grass, salt, and mildew. My eyes landed on the only real furniture in the place: two cots sitting across from each other with maybe only five feet of space between them, and a mirror hanging from a wooden support post. Thin-looking, navy gray blankets were folded neatly on top of each cot, their dull colors doing nothing to make the room feel more comfortable. A small wooden table was wedged into the far corner with a single chair pulled up beside it, its legs uneven on the old wooden floor.

"This is our room?" I froze in the doorway, staring at the setup like maybe if I'd spent enough time waiting, something else would appear. Something else. Literally anything else. My fingers tightened against the strap of my bag. "It's so…small and tiny."

"Don't be dramatic, Teachy," Marcus said, gesturing lazily toward the cots. His grin widened, like he was taking some private satisfaction in the fact that I'd just realized what this meant. "You'll survive. I don't bite."

My chest tightened at his words. I had prepared myself for sharing space with a stranger, someone I might barely have to interact with beyond passing hellos and occasional small talk. But I hadn't prepared for being crammed into a one-room hut with the guy who seemed to find me endlessly entertaining at my own expense. And somehow in the shock of seeing this broom closet in all its glory, it completely slipped my mind that

Marcus and I got to share this room for the next year or so.

The silence stretched between us once again, and as I stood there in the doorway, I couldn't make myself step further inside. The air between us felt heavier than the humidity, like the space itself was already too crowded with just us standing there.

I let out a laugh that sounded far too loud in the tiny space, hoping it would break the tension. "Sorry," I said quickly, rubbing the back of my neck. "Didn't mean anything by that. It's just been a while since I've had to share a room with someone. My college roommate snored like a wild animal! Not to mention, I'm just generally anxious about being around new people." My words sounded awkward even to me, like I was fumbling through a script I hadn't had time to rehearse. The words barely covered the unease crawling up my spine.

"Hey, no worries," Marcus leaned against the far wall, arms crossed, tilting his head slightly like he found my extreme levels of discomfort amusing. "I know how it is," he said casually, like sharing a room was nothing more than a minor inconvenience rather than some trial I hadn't expected. "But don't worry, I don't snore," he smirked.

"Yeah, don't worry about it! Sounds good!" I muttered in response, letting the words trail off into a nervous hum. My stomach churned again, not from sickness, but from anticipation. I hadn't slept in a room with anyone else since college, and even then, it had been temporary, controlled, with a party animal who was out every other night drinking. But this was different. I didn't know Marcus, I didn't *like* Marcus, and we were supposed to live here together, in this tiny space, for the next year on this island.

I swallowed hard and allowed myself to step fully into the room, letting the door click softly shut behind me. The warm, damp air pressed against my skin, carrying the faint smell of grass and salty water. I tried to focus on something tangible, something to occupy my mind before it inevitably went back to nonstop stress. My eyes eventually landed on the cot closest to me. The thin mattress looked harder than I expected, but I set my duffel bag down and took a seat next to it anyway. The bag thumped against the bed with a soft *thud*, the sound echoing a little in the small space.

I tugged the strap off my shoulder and let my hands rest on my knees. The mattress shifted beneath me with a creaky groan, and I tried to straighten my posture, pretending I wasn't acutely aware of Marcus standing confidently across the room, studying me like I was some weird human puzzle. Not that there was much else in the room he could be studying.

"What a nice little bed…" I gave the bed a small, half-hearted compliment, hoping the casual tone would mask my nerves. "Well, it's not terrible here. Kind of cozy," I said, letting the word hang awkwardly in the air. The mattress was firm, lumpy in places, and the thin blanket felt almost decorative, but saying anything else felt…wrong. The whole situation felt wrong.

Marcus didn't react immediately; he just leaned against the wall and watched me. His expression was calm, too calm, like he wasn't bothered by the tiny room at all. He never seemed to let anything bother him.

I felt my stomach twist again, partly from the heat and partly from realizing how long we'd stuck in this shared space together. "Yeah, we've got it made here for sure."

I ran a hand over the bed once again, smoothing out the wrinkles, trying to claim the tiny part of the tiny room as my own. Outside, faint laughter carried in from somewhere in the village, followed by the rhythmic clatter of dishes from a nearby kitchen. The sounds should have been comforting, a sign of life, love, and routine, but in that moment, they only highlighted how alone and awkward I felt. My mother was not there to cook me dinner. My friends weren't there to go with me for a burger at Sonic. Everything was now solely my responsibility. Everything was in my hands.

I shifted on my bed again, trying to find an angle on the thin mattress that would be the most comfortable to spend the next year or so. It was hard for me to get comfortable at all with Marcus being so close. Four feet didn't even sound like much, but in the small room, it felt almost like a chasm. Looking down at my feet, I noticed my duffel sat at my side. Running away didn't seem like such a bad idea still.

Marcus leaned forward slightly, resting one forearm across his knee. Then, without any ceremony, he extended his hand toward me. The motion was deliberate but relaxed, a small, kind gesture that completely caught me off guard.

"I'm sorry, I don't think I've formally introduced myself," he said, letting his hand hang there, waiting. "The name's Marcus Voss."

I blinked at him, caught between irritation, relief, and something else I couldn't quite name. Part of me wanted to refuse, to keep my distance, but the gesture demanded something, and I knew he was reading me just as closely as I was reading him. Slowly, I reached out and accepted his hand.

A firm shake, nothing too tight but confident enough to leave an impression. I offered a half smile, the kind that was more awkward than friendly. "Noah Ellison," I said, my voice almost cracking. I'd always been Noah Ellison, but I sounded so unsure of myself now.

He held my gaze for a moment, then released my hand and leaned back slightly on his cot, settling into a casual pose that made the room feel both smaller and bigger at the same time. I stayed where I was, still gripping the edge of my cot, aware that somehow, this simple handshake had shifted the dynamic of the room—maybe in a small way, maybe in a bigger one I couldn't see yet. It felt so weird holding an actual conversation with Marcus. Hearing words come out of him that weren't sarcasm.

Around us, the sun slanted through the small gaps in the walls, highlighting dust motes that hung lazily in the air. I glanced down at my duffel again, then back at Marcus, feeling the weight of our time ahead pressing quietly into the edges of my mind. We sat there facing each other, a silent acknowledgment passing between us that this was where things would start—awkward, tense, and uncomfortably close. *How much will I have to interact with him? Are there other huts I could move to? Why is he so comfortable around me?* All of these thoughts began speeding through my mind.

I shifted on the cot, tugging at the strap of my duffel again, though it didn't make any difference. Finally, I cleared my throat and said, "Uh… please excuse me. I'm still feeling a little sick from the plane. I think I need to get some fresh air… maybe explore the village a little. I'll be back later!" My voice sounded smaller than I intended, swallowed up by the cramped room and the hum of the thatched roof above us.

Marcus tilted his head and chuckled slightly but didn't give me too hard a look. "Of course," he said, almost too easily, like he already figured I'd need a few moments to recover from the awkwardness of the room.

I nodded, quickly grabbed my duffel again, and headed for the door. The latch clicked softly behind me as it shut and I stepped out into the sunlight. I sat down on the front step of the bure, my feet dangling just above the ground. I tried to square my shoulders, telling myself the same thing over and over: *It's fine. I'm fine. Everything's fine.* My eyes roamed the village—the row of bures along the edge, the narrow dirt paths winding between them, the occasional palm tree swaying in the breeze—but the words kept circling in my mind, demanding repetition.

It's fine. I'm fine. Everything's fine.

I whispered it out loud this time. I didn't feel a change, so I tried again, louder this time, like the motion of speaking louder might somehow convince the part of me that felt nervous, out of place, and suddenly very aware of how small I was in this world. Maybe if I said it enough, I'd believe it. Maybe the heat, the humidity, and the pounding of my pulse could be outrun by repetition.

Looking out on the village, the world felt so quiet now, almost deceptively so. A few children's voices carried faintly in the distance, laughter that seemed impossibly carefree compared to the tight coil in my stomach. I focused on the sound, on the rhythm of the breeze in the palms, on anything other than Marcus and the cot across from mine, waiting for me to return.

I hugged my knees closer, leaning back just enough to let the sun hit my face, trying to ground myself in the simple, mundane reality of this front step. If I could just sit here long enough, maybe I could trick myself into thinking I was safe, that I wasn't suddenly caught in a situation far bigger than I'd expected. Maybe I could convince myself I was still at home.

It's fine. I'm fine. Everything's fine.

The first step off the bure's front porch felt heavier than it should have. My feet sank slightly into the soft, dusty path, and the sun hammered down without mercy. I tried to keep my shoulders loose, telling myself it was just a walk, just a way to figure out the village, but every step felt like it was dragging me toward the future I wasn't ready for.

I started slowly, moving further down the dusty path, nodding at anyone I passed. The villagers were quiet at first, observing me with curiosity. A few smiled and waved, others kept their distance, going about their chores or carrying baskets of fresh produce in their arms. I forced myself to return the gestures, half-smiling, half-wincing at the sun and heat, but it felt necessary. I didn't want to be the awkward stranger in their small world.

I made my way toward what looked like the center of the village, where a cluster of simple buildings formed a kind of informal hub. There was a small market stand with colorful fruit stacked in huge piles and a few women weaving mats beside it. I paused for a moment to take it in, letting my eyes wander over the layout. Each path branched unpredictably, leading to homes, small gardens, or nothing but tall grass and the hint of forest beyond. If I needed any more proof this place wasn't home, I was looking at it.

Introducing myself proved to be harder than I'd thought. Everyone seemed too busy to want to hold a conversation with me. I tried introducing myself to several villagers, but the words caught in my throat sometimes, and my voice kept wavering in the heat. "Hi, I'm Noah," I said repeatedly, offering a handshake or a nod when someone seemed receptive. A few people returned the gesture with smiles or polite bows, and a couple of children giggled when I stumbled over my own pronunciation of the local words.

By mid-afternoon, the sun had turned the dirt paths into a hot, slow-burning heating pad. If I stepped in the wrong place, my feet felt like I was walking across a bed of hot coals. Even though I'd slipped my sweater off a couple minutes earlier, it had done nothing to help me cool down. My shirt stuck to my back, and sweat trickled down my sides, soaking the fabric. I kept moving, walking from one cluster of homes to another, trying to remember landmarks, the position of water sources, and the small communal buildings that might serve as gathering spots. Every step was heavier than the last.

I eventually ducked under a low tree to get some shade, suck in some cool breaths, and compose myself once again. My knees wobbled slightly, and I had to pause, gripping the trunk to keep myself upright. Standing in the sun all day had left me dizzy, a reminder that I never got the chance to fully acclimatize to this climate.

I eventually forced myself forward, deciding to resume my walk through the village. I filled the next hour by taking my time introducing my name to villagers once again, asking simple questions about their lives, and helping some people carry supplies from one place to another, the whole time letting my curiosity try to outweigh my growing fatigue. Every interaction helped take the heat off my mind. But in the end, my shirt was still soaked, my lips still dry, and the sun still constantly burned my neck, but I kept telling myself that moving, learning, seeing—it was all worth it. Even if I didn't totally believe it.

It's fine. I'm fine. Everything's fine.

By late afternoon, I found myself slumping against the edge of another building, my legs trembling beneath me. After all the exploring I'd done, I had a rough mental map of the village, or at least enough to feel less like a completely lost stranger. But my day's work had come at a troubling cost. My skin felt raw from the sun and sweat, my shirt clung uncomfortably as it was now fully soaked, and I realized my energy was almost completely gone.

I sank to the ground, trying to catch my breath, feeling the heat radiate up from the dirt beneath me. The village was alive all around, but I couldn't stop noticing how every step, every interaction, was draining me, leaving me brittle and a little desperate for shade, water, and the safety of my home.

My eyes wandered out through the village, taking in the paths I had walked just hours before, the clusters of bures, the garden plots where someone was tending crops, and the faint shimmer of the distant coastline. That's when I noticed him again. Marcus.

He was a few yards away, crouched slightly, laughing in that easy, careless way that made me so envious. Around him, a small group of children darted and ran, chasing a ball that had been improvised from scraps of fabric and twine. Marcus clapped his hands, encouraged them, ducked, and dodged, moving with a rhythm that seemed to belong to him completely. His smile was wide, genuine, unguarded, and it struck me in a way I hadn't expected.

I blinked and looked again, thinking maybe my tired eyes were playing tricks on me, but there was no illusion. He was happy. Completely, unconcernedly happy. How had he done it? There was no shadow of fatigue or homesickness in the way he interacted with the kids, no hint that he was longing for a familiar home, a familiar bed, or the voices of his family. It was like this place had always been his home.

I shifted against the wall, trying to understand, trying to reconcile the image of him here—so alive, so effortlessly at ease. With everything I thought I knew about being far from home, about being stranded in a place where every face was foreign and every path unknown, he wasn't bothered at all. The sunlight hit his hair, catching in the strands in a way that made him seem almost untouchable, and a part of me resented it. He was so comfortable being himself here, it was almost attractive. How could someone be so… content, when I was struggling just to exist here?

I hugged my knees closer, my arms shaking slightly from exhaustion and frustration. The sounds of the game carried faintly to me—the children's laughter, Marcus's voice, and the scuff of feet against the dirt. It was a strange, foreign music, one I couldn't quite step into. I wanted to understand it, to feel even a fraction of that ease, but I couldn't.

Opening my eyes again, I let the sun and the sounds wash over me, trying to convince myself that I wasn't envious, that I could figure out how to survive here. He had no problem living a carefree life here because he didn't have a life like mine. He didn't work as hard as I did to get here, and there was no way he had a family as great as mine. I wasn't envious; he was just ignorant.

Chapter Five

I woke to the sound of waves crashing on the shore in the distance. The noise of people nearby had kept me awake last night. I'd hoped to sleep better, to think more clearly about whether I wanted to stay or go home.

I turned over and saw that Marcus was still asleep on his cot. He was cuddling his pillow, and I wondered if he'd wake up with neck pain. For a moment, it didn't even look like he was breathing; he just laid there, motionless. Then, I heard an abrupt snore, so I knew he was alive.

I got out of bed, got dressed, and grabbed an orange to eat while I walked toward the academy. Fiji had some of the freshest fruits compared to the pallets of fruits that were imported to the grocery stores back home. Victor had some extra classroom supplies that he offered me, so we planned to set up my classroom together. When I arrived at the academy, Victor was waiting for me outside of the front office. He handed me my badge and a keychain of keys. I looked at the picture on my badge and laughed. It was the same photo I used for my college ID card. An oldie but a goldie.

"Good morning," Victor said.

"Hey," I replied.

"There's your badge for the copier and to get into the building, and the keys will unlock just about everything in your classroom."

"I'm excited."

"Shall we go to your room?"

"Sure," I said with a smile.

Victor led me into the front office where I met the secretary. I was given a brief tour before we exited out a side door to a fenced area where most of the classrooms were. We walked toward classroom 121, with "Mr. Ellison" printed outside the door. It was very heartwarming to see my name on the wall. I was no longer the student; I was the teacher.

"Here we are," Victor said. "You can do the honors of opening your classroom for the first time."

I took the keychain out of my pocket and inserted the key into the lock. The door opened, and I was met with humid air that felt like it was trapped inside for weeks.

"Maintenance must not have turned on the air conditioning. Let's get some windows open, and I will call them to turn it on," Victor said.

When we both stood inside, I took a look around. There was nothing. Just a bunch of desks stacked in the back of the room, a teacher's desk with an antiquated computer and telephone, and dim fluorescent lights on the ceiling. The rest was up to me. Since I was only teaching for the summer, I was told not to worry too much about decorating my classroom. As long as I taught my students, that was what mattered most. All I brought with me from America was a desk plate that said "Mr. Ellison."

Victor pointed to a box in the back corner of the room, where the light could not fill, and said that it was full of just about everything I would need to get started. We spent the next hour unstacking desks, setting up the computer, getting the room aired out, and organizing the materials that Victor had for me.

After we finished up, I went to the beach to think about what else I could do in my classroom to create a more enriching environment for my students. As I sat on the beach, I started to miss home. I thought about what I was missing in America. I thought about how I would probably be taking the street car around San Francisco, jumping off at a few stops to do some shopping with some friends.

A few hours later, I heard the sound of someone walking up behind me. I turned around and saw Victor with two colorful drinks in his hands.

"Here," he said, handing the drink to me before sitting down in the sand. "Don't get dehydrated out here. It'll make you sick."

"Thank you," I replied. "What kind of drink is this? It's a pretty color."

"It's a combination of lemon-lime soda with blue-raspberry and strawberry syrup."

"It tastes great!"

"So, what are you doing out here? Is everything alright?"

"Yeah, everything is fine. I just miss home more than I anticipated. I don't know if I can be away for this long."

"That's understandable. Our enrollment has decreased, so if you prefer to return home, we can get you on the plane that comes in about a week."

"What about the kids?"

"A few kids dropped out of our summer program, so the remaining ones that would be in your class can be shifted into other classes."

I sat there for a few moments, trying to decide whether I truly wanted to go home, or if I was just experiencing some slight home-sickness that would dissolve over the coming days.

"Can I have some time to think about it?" I asked Victor.

"Of course. Take your time. You know where to find me," Victor replied.

The sun was about to set, and Victor got up and walked away. I walked back to my cot, as I just wanted some alone time. When I got back, Marcus was not there. He was probably off flirting with one of the women from the village—he seemed like the type who always needed someone's attention. I laid in my bed, rolled over to the side opposite of the window, and quickly fell asleep.

— — — — — — — —

I woke up about an hour later, and the sun had set over the water. It was now almost dark, and I could hear Marcus approaching the hut. He fiddled with the key before opening the door and having it bang into the wall. He closed it before walking toward his bed. He saw me laying there, but I didn't think he could tell I was awake.

My eyes were open just barely enough that I saw his silhouette undress before getting into his bed. He rolled over a few times, and that's the last thing I remember before sleep took over.

Chapter Six

The sun felt heavier in the sky now. I could feel the rays soaking into every inch of skin, dragging me deeper into the sand until it felt like the island itself was breathing, trying to consume me as I lay on the shore. I let my eyes fall half-shut, and watched as the world above me blur into a field of light and lazy shapes. The sounds around me were calming: the swoosh of the tide creeping closer, the faint laughter of the village children somewhere beyond the beach, and the quiet rustle of palm fronds blowing in the wind.

I'd told Marcus I was going for a walk, but I hadn't gone far. I never did. What was the point? The beach had become a sort of refuge, a place that didn't ask anything of me. A place that didn't confine me to a single room. Just the warmth, the sand, and the comfort of being still. For the first time in a while, I was relaxed. I could lay here and just breathe.

I heard his footsteps before I saw him. They were slow and careful, like he didn't want to disturb me but also didn't trust me to be left alone here in the sand. When his shadow finally fell over me, I cracked one eye open and saw him standing there, the light cutting sharp across his features. His hair was untamed, probably from the wind, and his sleeves were rolled up to his elbows. He looked out toward the horizon and crossed his arms as he stood there in silence for a few moments. "You're gonna burn if you stay like that," he said finally.

"Maybe I want to," I muttered—too lazy to move.

He made a sound—half laugh, half sigh—and crouched down beside me, his knees leaving small craters in the sand. He pulled something from his pocket, and I caught the smell of it before I saw it: sunscreen. He held it out to me. "You should at least put this on," he said. "Unless you like looking like a boiled crab."

I smirked up at him from my place in the sand. For a moment, it felt like we were the only two people in the whole village. I sat up, took the small bottle from him, and let my fingers brush against his just long enough for him to notice. We didn't get to stay that way for long. A voice called out from up the hill, sharp and distant, cutting through the soft crash of the waves. Marcus looked toward the sound, then at me, and I already knew what he was going to say before he opened his mouth. “They’re calling for us,” he said. “I think we’d better go.”

I squinted toward the direction of the village. Even from here I could see them: bright fabric tents set up in a circle and a few villagers moving around in color-coordinating T-shirts. A banner strung between two trees read something about *unity* and *bonding*, the paint already starting to drip from the humidity. The whole thing looked ridiculous.

“What are they doing?” I muttered. “Is this some kind of bonding activity? You’d think surviving in the same one-room hut would count as bonding enough.”

“Looks like a bonding thing to me.” Marcus didn’t argue. He just waited until I finally dragged myself to my feet. The walk back was slow, the sand clung stubbornly to my clothes. Every few steps, I looked up at the sky and silently begged it to start raining, storming, or to do anything that might get us out of this.

By the time we reached the village square, the setup was already in full swing. Wooden crates had been stacked into small towers, ropes coiled neatly beside them, and someone was drawing crude chalk lines into the dirt. The villagers had divided themselves into groups, talking in low voices that carried just enough for me to hear snippets of their conversations. Things like "trust fall" and "challenge" seemed to be the rumors spread about.

Marcus greeted a few of them, while I lingered near the edge of the clearing, pretending to be interested in a piece of driftwood stuck in the ground. Someone, maybe the person responsible for this organization, clapped their hands for attention. "Pairs will be assigned shortly!" he called out. "Remember, this is all about connection and teamwork. Let's see how strong our bonds really are!"

I glanced at Marcus. He was already looking at me. "Don't say it," I warned.

"What do you mean?" He grinned. "Say what?"

"That we're doing this together," I said. "Or worse, that you think this'll be good for us."

He shrugged, doing a poor job of hiding his amusement. "Well… maybe it will be."

I groaned, loud enough for him to laugh. But even through the annoyance, I couldn't help noticing how he looked so relaxed. Even if I wasn't at peace, he sure seemed to be. I told myself that maybe that was reason enough to stay and play along—for him, if not for me. Still, when the instructor started walking over with a clipboard, I felt my stomach sink. Whatever this "bonding exercise" was going to be, I already hated it.

Sure enough, the instructor wasn't just anyone, it was Victor. Figures. He stood in the middle of the clearing with his usual air of forced enthusiasm, clipboard tucked under one arm and a whistle hanging from his neck like he was about to lead a summer camp of elementary school kids.

"Alright, everyone, listen up!" Victor called out, "Today's exercise is all about teamwork and trust. You've all started working hard getting yourselves set up, but now it's time to show how you function as pairs and as a team."

I leaned toward Marcus and muttered, "What's this gonna be, a trust fall into the mud?"

Victor pointed at me without even looking. "Noah, since I've noticed you two have been getting along so much better, I'm happy to announce that you and Marcus will be working together today."

Marcus smirked, clearly trying not to laugh, while I just groaned under my breath. "Lucky us," I said.

Victor continued on, flipping through pages on his clipboard. "The goal is simple. Each pair will be tied together at the wrist and will have to navigate through a short obstacle course. Nothing too dangerous, just a few balance logs, some rope climbing, and a little puzzle at the end. The idea is to move as one, think as one, and support each other without losing patience."

"Losing patience," I repeated quietly. "That'll be easy."

"I don't think you've had any patience since you got here." Marcus nudged my arm. "Come on, it could be fun."

I gave him a look. "You and I have very different definitions of fun."

Victor started handing out lengths of coarse rope, already paired off with each duo of villagers. He reached us last, possibly on purpose. "You two should be naturals at this," he said, tying the rope around our wrists with a grin that was way too confident. "You guys have been forming a great bond as roommates already!"

"Yeah, I'm sure we'll do great," I muttered not-so-confidently.

"Remember," he went on, stepping back to address the whole group again, "communication is key! If one of you stumbles, the other needs to help them up. If one gets frustrated, you both fail. You succeed together or not at all. It's all about teamwork!"

Marcus looked at me and smiled. "Well," he said, testing the rope between our wrists, "Guess we're stuck with each other for now," he said.

"Guess so," I replied, already seeing the two of us tripping over logs and eating dirt in front of everyone.

Around us, the other pairs were talking, laughing, and practicing walking in sync. I just stared down at the knot around my wrist, the fibers rough against my skin, and tried to tell myself it wouldn't be as bad as I thought. But then Victor blew the whistle, the sound sharp and way too cheerful, and my stomach began to sink all over again.

"Go!" Victor shouted, clapping his hands. "Teamwork!"

"Yeah, yeah," I muttered, tugging Marcus forward through the jungle path.

Victor had marked the trees of the jungle along the course with bright yellow paint, and the path we followed was only wide enough for maybe two people, so therc was no room for error in this contest. There were already two groups ahead of us, so we had to move fast.

The first obstacle was a long log bridge spanning over a shallow stream. Easy enough normally, if we weren't tied together and both wearing shoes with socks that felt like sponges from the sweat and humidity. Marcus led us up on the log and the two of us struggled for a moment to balance. "Left foot," Marcus said. "Then right."

"I can walk without instructions," I said, right before I stepped too early and yanked him forward. The log wobbled under our combined weight, both of us windmilling our arms to stay balanced. The pair ahead of us had already made it across and were halfway through to the next obstacle beyond the stream.

"Easy there!" Marcus caught his footing and glared at me, but he didn't say anything. We shuffled the rest of the way, awkwardly just out of sync, and nearly toppled off when we reached solid ground.

The next obstacle was worse, a wall made of wooden slats, maybe eight feet high, with a dangling rope on each side. Marcus reached for it first, gripping tight, but when he started to climb, the rope jerked me forward so fast my forehead hit the wood. "Ow!"

"Sorry!" he said.

"Just keep climbing before I lose consciousness," I grunted, rubbing my head.

We managed to scramble up and over the wall, even if our movements were clumsy and uncoordinated. My sleeve caught on a nail at the top, and I had to twist awkwardly to free it while Marcus tried not to fall off the other side. By the time we jumped down, my wrist was raw from the rope rubbing between us. "This is hurting, this is hurting!"

"You guys are all doing great!" Victor yelled from somewhere behind us. "Just one last obstacle in the course!"

The third obstacle looked like it was designed by someone who hated fun. It was a series of stepping stones across a muddy pit, spaced just far enough apart to make coordination nearly impossible. The rocks seemed to be in a random pattern that lacked any rhyme or reason. There was no sign of the groups ahead of us, somehow they'd made it across in no time.

"I don't understand, how could anyone make those jumps?" I asked aloud. "This doesn't make sense."

"Wait a second, Noah. Look!" Marcus called, pointing at the stepping stones. "Certain rocks are positioned just close enough across from each other to jump diagonally. That's what makes it a puzzle, we just have to choose the right ones!"

I was confused, I saw no difference in the placement of any of the rocks. They all looked the same, and none of them made any promise of a safe landing. "Uh… I'm not so sure."

"Okay," Marcus said, breathing hard. "We'll jump together."

"Yeah. Yeah, okay," I said, "what could possibly go wrong?"

We jumped, and what went wrong was everything. Marcus landed cleanly. I didn't. My foot slid off the second stone we reached, and before I could regain my balance, I pulled him down with me into the mud. It was cold and thick, swallowing us both up to our knees. The rope kept us tangled, and by the time we clawed our way back out, every other team (and Victor) had already crossed the obstacle. The two of us made our way shamefully out of the jungle and back to the village clearing.

Victor's whistle blew again. "Great job, everyone!" he announced. "Looks like Noah and Marcus are bringing up the rear!"

"Totally planned." I wiped mud from my face, glaring through it at Victor. "We were going for dramatic effect," I said.

We stood there before the rest of the group, dripping with mud and water, the rope between us stretched tight. Everyone else was catching their breath and congratulating each other, and Victor was making notes on his clipboard. We seemed to be the only two having trouble getting along here. Or at the very least, we were the only two that had problems faking it.

Marcus laughed, "Yeah," he said. "Noah insisted we go easy on everyone. But that ends now!"

"That's the spirit! You guys will do much better with the next one, I'm sure!" he called out cheerfully.

I looked at Marcus, then at the swampy mess behind us. "Hang on, hang on. Next one?"

He just shrugged, smiling through the mud. “Hey, we can only improve from here, right?” He may have been confident, but I definitely was not.

Victor blew the whistle again, and everyone lined up at the starting point, including me and Marcus, still dripping and streaked with mud. The rope connecting Marcus and me was shorter this time, and tied around our ankles. Victor said it was to encourage us to “Walk with each other’s shoes,” but think it was more likely just sabotage.

“Alright!” Victor barked, grinning with all his teeth. “Second round! Remember—focus, trust, and coordination! You’ve got to move as one!”

“Easier said than done,” I muttered.

Marcus looked over at me, half-smiling. “We got this,” he said. “One step at a time.”

“Right,” I replied with a smile, already bracing myself for disaster.

The next obstacle course was seemingly much more simple. It consisted of only a line of barrels that each had to cross by stepping on top and rolling them forward with our feet. The pair ahead of us—Savenaca and one of the young fishermen from the village—moved like they’d been practicing for weeks, gliding across in perfect harmony. They belonged out here, they were in their element. Meanwhile, Marcus and I were too busy arguing about which direction to roll to make any progress. Together we hopped up onto the first barrel and prepared for the worst as we started moving.

"Left foot first!" I told him.

"No, your right foot—!" he yelled.

Finally, the barrel slipped out from under us, and I hit the ground hard, pulling Marcus down with me. He landed flat beside me with a loud "oof," and for a second we both just stared at the sky, mud splattering our faces once again. My back ached from the fall and I didn't feel like getting up again.

Victor blew his whistle. "Remember! Teamwork means communication!"

"Yeah," I said under my breath. "We know."

"Well," Marcus chuckled, wiping his face. "Maybe we should just crawl to the finish line this time."

We got up to make another attempt, this time in an effort to manage and stay upright long enough to barely get across. It was a slow, awkward dance of close calls and muttered curses. My calves were burning, and Marcus kept apologizing for pulling too hard or stepping too soon as the rope burned against my ankle. We were only a couple barrels away before anything went too wrong.

"Wait, stop, don't pull!" I said.

"I'm not pulling, you're pulling!" he yelled.

Suddenly, the knot at our feet gave way, and we tumbled backward off the barrels and into the dirt, both of us sprawled on our backs, staring up at the palm fronds swaying overhead.

Victor's whistle blew one last time as Marcus and I stepped back into the clearing. "And that's it for round two! Once again, Noah and Marcus bring up the rear. And that's okay!"

A few people clapped politely, though I couldn't tell if it was for encouragement or pity. Although deep down I could tell it was pity. I groaned and sat up, brushing dirt off my arms and legs.

"Second-to-last next time," I said. "That's our new goal."

Marcus grinned. "It's a start!"

Victor walked over, clipboard still in hand, "You two have spirit," he said. "That's something!"

"Yeah," I said, "spirit, mud, and minor injuries."

Marcus laughed at me under his breath, and despite myself, I couldn't help but smile too. We started back toward the group, our steps uneven with each other but with a little more rhythm than before. If only we were still tethered together.

Victor gathered us all again at the third and final starting line, the sun beginning to dip behind the trees in the distance. The air was heavy with heat and salt, dirt and sand clinging to every inch of me. I could feel the tension in the air. "Final round, everyone!" Victor called out. "Give it your all!"

Marcus and I exchanged a glance. For once, he looked serious and focused. No jokes, no smirk. Like he actually wanted to prove something. "Let's do it right this time," he said. "We've got this."

"Right," I said, smiling. Our opposite arms were now the only thing tied together. Our arms were bound together from our forearm to our shoulder. "Just… try not to get us deep in the mud this time."

The whistle blew, sharp and echoing across the village. We bolted forward as soon as the sound hit our ears. We were in the lead for once, and we weren't going to give it up. "Let's go!" Marcus shouted.

After a few minutes running along the path, we hit the final obstacle—a wall of netting strung between two posts. A sort of makeshift monkey bars of ropes suspended over a torrent river. We climbed fast, almost perfectly in sync now. My hands slipped once, but Marcus caught the tension in the rope before I could fall, keeping us both steady. By the time we reached the middle of the crossing, I looked beside me and grinned at him.

"Nice save!" I said. "We're actually doing it!"

He smiled back. "Don't get used to it!"

After a short while, we dropped down on the other side, hitting the sand hard but balanced. Several teams were catching up behind us, but we still had enough distance to make it for the win. For once, it felt like maybe, just maybe, we were actually working well together. "Nicely done, Noah!"

I nodded, letting him move first. We found a rhythm, stepping carefully, our weight shifting together against our arms. Victor and the crowd of villagers started cheering in the distance, some for us, some for others, I couldn't tell, but for the first time since this whole thing started, I didn't feel like we were hopeless.

We reached the final stretch, a sprint through shallow water to a bright blue flag post at the end of the path. It was a small cove nestled in a secret section of beach where Victor and the villagers waited for us all. The sun flashed off the waves, and the salt burned my legs, but it didn't matter. We were catching up.

"Go, go, go!" I shouted. "We can make it!"

We ran, water splashing everywhere, our strides matching. We were actually closing the gap. Savenaca and his teammate were only a few dozen feet behind us. Marcus laughed breathlessly, "We might actually win this thing!"

"Don't jinx it!" I yelled, though I couldn't help but laugh too.

Then, just as we were nearly twenty feet from the finish, the rope between us snagged on a lowhanging branch and pulled us back. We stumbled, and before I could stop, the tension pulled me off balance. We both went down hard, crashing into the shallow surf. The flag waved mockingly above us as Savenaca and his partner tore past, cheering and whooping.

By the time we got back on our feet, soaked and gasping, the race was over. Victor was already clapping for the winners. Marcus bent over, hands on his knees, breathing hard. "So close," he muttered. "We were so close!

"Yeah," I said, brushing water off my arms. "Story of our lives."

Victor jogged over, smiling like he'd seen this coming all along. The rest of the villagers and competitors cheered for Savenaca and his partner. "You two were looking good out there," he said. "Almost perfect that time. What happened?"

"I'm not sure." Marcus gave a tired laugh. "I think the world is just working against us."

"Ah," Victor said, raising a brow. "Well, I know sometimes it feels like that." He clapped Marcus on the shoulder, then mine. "The important thing is that you two know the power you have together."

We stood there in the surf for a while thinking about what he said, the water lapping at our ankles. Marcus shook his head, still smiling faintly.

"Next time," he said.

"Sure," I said, smirking. "Next time maybe we'll come in second."

By the time we all trudged back toward the village, every muscle in my body was screaming. My arms and legs were caked in sand, mud, and sweat. My shirt stuck to my chest like glue and was in a state beyond repair. Marcus was just as bad, his hair plastered to his forehead, his arms scraped from the logs and netting.

We stopped near the edge of the village, breathing hard, water dripping from our clothes, and looked at each other. I could see the same exhaustion mirrored in his eyes. He leaned against a tree, shaking his head before dropping to his knees. "Never… ever… again," he said, his voice ragged. "Whatever we do together, please don't let it be an obstacle course."

I gave a weak laugh, dropping to the sand and sitting beside him. "Agreed. We are never working together in one of Victor's exercises ever again."

He wiped his hands over his face, smearing dirt across his cheeks. It was almost cute. "I thought we had a shot that last round… I thought we'd almost had it."

"Almost," I echoed, rolling my shoulders. "That's the problem. Almost isn't enough."

He chuckled dryly, shaking his head. "Next time, we'll just avoid him completely and go work together on getting some pizza or something."

I smirked despite my tiredness. "Sounds perfect."

"Agreed," he said. Nothing else needed to be said. We both knew it; it was undeniable: teamwork was officially off the table.

Chapter Seven

I woke up in what must have been the middle of the night and looked out our window, noticing the sky was a dark gray color. The sight made me feel sad. It didn't help that I already felt grayer than the skies with everything else going on. After a moment of rustling around, Marcus woke up as I propped myself up. I accidentally dropped my phone on the floor.

"Sorry," I said.

"You're fine," he responded. "Don't worry about it."

Knowing I'd never get back to sleep, I decided to start my morning, getting ready for the day, eating a granola bar, and walking outside to take in the fresh air. It looked like it had rained overnight; the ground was wet, and the trees were dripping. I was surprised that I slept through it. The noise would have most likely awakened me.

After spending some time outside waking myself up, absorbing the views of sparkling blue water, I walked my sandy feet back into our bure to finish getting ready for the day. I didn't really have any plans, but I was hoping I'd get the chance to take some pictures to show everyone back home in California. As I walked back into the bure. Marcus had seemingly fallen back asleep, snoring just louder than the waves crashing on the shore. I managed to quietly make my way to the mirror hanging in the corner of the room to examine the state of my hair. As I was combing my hair, a knock pounded on the door of our bure.

"Can you get that," Marcus mumbled. "I'm so tired…"

"Yeah," I said, walking over to the door and hesitantly opening it. *Who was knocking on doors at this hour?* Standing in front of me was an older man, thin and balding, his hair silver and unkept. His beard was tangled and full of knots. He looked like as big a wreck as I felt.

"Please help me," he said, his hands shaking, holding an empty plastic bag that was blowing in the wind. "I need your help!"

"Of course," I said. "What's going on?"

"I was moving stuff along the beach, and some of it fell into the water, and the current is taking it out. I have to get on my boat to get it, but I can't do it alone. Some of the stuff is too heavy for me." The man seemed panicked, his breathing was quick and shallow. "Nobody in the village is as young and strong as you two, I could really use your help."

"Of course. We will help you." I turned my head to Marcus, who was still half asleep behind me. "Marcus, we need your help. Some supplies fell into the water."

"Ugh, fine," Marcus said as he sat up in bed, stretching his arms. He reluctantly pulled himself out of bed and stood up, grabbing a folded piece of paper from under his pillow as he stood. I didn't think he knew that I knew what it was, a letter that had been given to him by Victor earlier in the day. I'm not sure what it'd said, but ever since he got it, Marcus had been in a sour mood. "Let's go."

Marcus quickly got ready and met me and the older man outside of the bure. We walked down to a little boat that looked like it would sink if all three of us got in. But despite our hesitation, the man pushed us into the tiny space and untied us from the dock. We began paddling maybe 10 yards out toward two small crates floating in the water. The more we paddled, the farther out the items seemed to be. Like we were not getting closer. "The current is pulling everything further out!" I yelled over the waves, "Maybe we should turn back!"

"We'll be fine!" The old man yelled, "We're almost there."

As we continued further out, heavy rain began to pour over us. I couldn't speak for the old man who was guiding us, but I could not see anything in front of us. Or behind us for that matter. The sky became dark, the only thing illuminating it was the occasional flash of lightning.

"We need to turn back," I said to the old man as I adjusted my glasses. "We're not gonna make it!"

"We *can* make it," he replied. "We're almost there!"

"We're not, though!" Marcus shouted to him. "I'm not dying out here for three crates of junk!"

The old man looked beyond offended at Marcus's words. "It's not junk! There's bibles in those boxes! For you to do your job!"

"Well now I feel bad about yelling! Carry on then!" Marcus yelled.

I grew anxious as the thunder grew louder around us and the waves became larger. Between the rain and the waves, our boat was slowly collecting water inside. With how small and fragile the boat was, I was afraid we would end up in the water. We didn't have life jackets on, but these waves were so intense that I'm not sure if that would have mattered anyway.

By pure coincidence, we finally happened upon the supplies floating in the open water. We pulled all three crates into the boat and began paddling back toward the shore. Since we couldn't see much of anything in front of us, we had to hope we were going the right direction. The only thing guiding us was the faint lights from the village, but even through the rain, they were almost nothing.

Within the first five minutes of the journey back, the waves became increasingly rough. The boat shook and kept nearly tipping as we rowed. Marcus and I used all our strength to fight against the tide, trying to keep our boat upright. Abruptly, a wave crashed into the side of us strong enough that it knocked the old man right into the water.

"Help me!" The old man yelled, his screams almost drowned out by the thunder.

"We have to help him!" I shouted. "Marcus, do something!"

"What do you want me to do?! It's way too rough out here!" We couldn't see the man and we tried calling out for him, but there was no response. No yells, no screams, nothing.

"Marcus, we can't just leave him out here," I said. "We need to find him."

"What can we do?" he asked. "We don't have life jackets. What's the point of us going in the water?"

"We aren't that far away from the shore now, maybe only 100 yards? I think we can swim back." I took off my glasses and stuffed them into my pocket. "You stay here and guide the boat back to the village. I'm going in after him."

"Are you crazy?!" Marcus asked.

I didn't respond. Instead, I looked over the side of the boat and prepared to jump in. The waves were crazy and the water was rough. The water looked like a black abyss below us, ready to swallow me whole. The weight of fear pulled my back into the boat, refusing to let me anywhere near the edge again. "I can't…"

"Good," Marcus said. "There's no way you'd make it back to shore. Not alive."

"Then you save him!" I pleaded, "You Christians don't just let people die, right? Get in there!"

Marcus looked at me, blank face, like I'd just told him a bad joke. "First of all, I'm Catholic, not Christian. And second of all, no! I'm not dying to maybe save someone I don't even know!"

I felt awful leaving the guy out in the ocean alone, but there wasn't anything more I could do. I was too afraid to jump in. And Marcus was probably right, it was a huge risk. Whose to say we could even do anything to save him? We were barely able to stay afloat, so we knew we had no time to waste in getting back to the island.

Suddenly, a strong wave crashed into the side of the boat again, and Marcus and I almost fell into the water. We toppled on top of each other in a small pile in the middle of our craft. I looked down and saw water was starting to fill the inside, faster now.

"Marcus, I'm scared. I don't think the boat will get us back to shore. It is filling up with water."

"It's gonna have to hold!" Marcus said, "We're way too far out to swim back in these waters!"

"Well we're gonna have to swim back," I replied. "The boat's not gonna hold!"

Marcus seemed to think to himself for a moment. He looked at me, and then at the water. Nodding. "I think it's our only choice. We have to abandon ship."

"I thought you said we'd never be able to swim back?!" I protested.

"I did…" he began, looking at the sky as it continued to pour rain over us. "But the boat's just going to keep pulling us further out. We have to go."

Seeing the worry in his eyes and the determination in his posture, I didn't fight back. I trusted him. "Okay."

Marcus turned to me, grabbed my hand, and seemed to mentally prepare for us to jump out into the water. My heartbeat pounded in my ears, just as loud as the thunder and waves around us. My anxiety was skyrocketing. I squeezed Marcus's hand tighter.

Just as we were about to jump out of the boat, another wave crashed into us, forcing us out. The water was ice cold, and the waves felt even rougher than before. Every couple of seconds water rushed over my head, trying to pull me under.

"Are you ok?!" I asked, looking around. "Marcus?!"

"Yeah, I'm fine," Marcus responded, swimming up next to me. "I'm right here."

"I'm scared, Marcus," I began. "What if we can't make it back?"

Marcus put a hand on my shoulder. "We will. I know we will."

We paddled some more, but it wasn't enough. Every inch we got closer to the village, the further the current seemed to pull us out. As I began to take a moment to breathe, the water swallowed me whole without warning. I kicked hard, fighting against the pull of the tide, the salt water stinging my eyes as I tried to figure out which way was up. My lungs screamed in agony, and for a second I thought this might be the end. I'd never see anything again.

Then, through the haze, I saw a flash of light, bright and huge, streaking across the sky. Lightning. I lunged toward it. My head broke the surface with a gasp so sharp it burned my throat. I spun around, blinking through the spray of the waves. The boat was gone. Marcus was gone. The rain became heavier, making the sky look wrong, like the clouds had melted into the water. Every direction was the same dull gray, and I shouted, "Marcus?!"

"Marcus!" I shouted again, my throat raw. No response. The waves rolled me sideways, and I swallowed a mouthful of saltwater that burned as I swallowed it. Panic hit harder than the current. Then, just barely, I heard it. A yell, faint and hoarse. Marcus was calling my name.

I turned toward the sound and spotted him a few yards away. He looked rough and scared, his dark hair plastered to his face. I swam toward him, my arms heavy, legs trembling with each kick. When I finally reached him, we clung to each other, barely keeping our heads above the surface.

"We just have to keep swimming," he said between gasps of air. "The current's got to push us somewhere."

"Somewhere?" I coughed. "We don't even know where we are! It could bring us anywhere!"

As Marcus began to reply, another wave smacked into us, splitting us briefly before we locked arms again. The cold wind cut like glass against my skin. My fingers were going numb. I tried to focus on calming down, but everything around us was in chaos.

Minutes—or maybe even whole hours—passed as we swam. We swam without knowing if it mattered, if we were moving forward or just turning in circles. My arms ached, my chest burned, and every thought I had blurred into the same desperate plea to stay above water. We paddled some more, but it wasn't enough. I couldn't keep paddling anymore. I was ready for the current to bring me somewhere. Anywhere.

Chapter Eight

After what must have been hours, I awoke to the taste of salt in the air, more so than in the village, with the endless sound of waves pounding against the sand. After a couple of moments, my eyes snapped open, squinting against the blinding sun reflecting off the water, and I realized I was lying flat on my back. Every part of me ached—my arms, my legs, my shoulders—but the sand beneath me felt cool and sticky against my skin. “What happened?” I groaned. “Are we back on the shore?” There was no answer. *Marcus? Marcus!* My mind started racing as I worried about his safety.

I slowly rolled to my side, testing my balance, trying not to move too quickly in case my body decided to revolt. My lungs filled with the heavy, humid air, and I swallowed hard, tasting nothing but sand and salt. I looked around and saw the storm had left more than just a few broken branches, the remains of our boat, and ourselves in its wake.

My gaze followed the large curve of the shoreline, scanning for something familiar. Anything familiar. Nothing looked like the place we had landed in, nothing looked like the village we were assigned to. Trees lined the coast in thick, tangled clusters, their roots gripping the sand and mud as if holding on for dear life, and the jungle beyond the beach was dark, dense, and uninviting. I shivered despite the warmth of the sun, my teeth chattering slightly, and I tried to push myself up with my hands, only to realize they were trembling beyond control. As much as I wanted out of that village, I'd give anything to go back now.

I brushed some of the sand off my clothes, shaking my arms and legs like I could dislodge the aches that worked their way throughout my body. The sun was already high above me, burning through the remnants of storm clouds, and I could feel its heat on my back, relentless and harsh.

I began looking around for my glasses. They were nowhere in sight. A couple of yards away, there lay Marcus, like a beached whale that had washed up on the shore. As I trudged over to him, my feet sank deeper into the wet sand with every step, making the walk toward him slower than it should have been. It didn't help that I already felt like falling over and dying right there. My troubles would have ended a lot sooner if I did.

When I got to him, I crouched beside him and shouted his name, loud enough that the entire stretch of beach could hear it. “Marcus!” My voice cracked the first time, my throat salty and dry. So I tried again, sharper, more desperate, “Marcus, wake up!” I yelled, the salty taste of panic now heavy in my mouth. When he still didn’t move, my patience finally wavered and I decided my best option was to kick some sand at him. It flew up in a cloud, settling on his clothes, his face, and still, he didn’t move. My heart sank when I realized he may not have been as lucky as me to wake up after the storm.

He finally groaned, lifting his head just enough to squint at me. His eyes were bleary, his hair plastered to his forehead from the sweat and saltwater. “What… happened?” he muttered, voice rough and heavy, dragging itself out of sleep like it didn’t want to be awake either. “Did we make it back to the village?”

“What happened?” I took a step back, throwing up my hands in frustration. “What happened?! We’re stranded! Who knows where we are! Who knows where the storm took us!” I yelled, before realizing for a moment I had to stop and just watch him. He blinked at me slowly, processing. For someone that just got shipwrecked, he seemed pretty unbothered.

Marcus shifted slightly, trying to stand up but legs still wobbly. The storm's toll was clearly heavy on his body too. My pulse was pounding in my ears, loud enough that I could barely hear the faint crash of the waves in front of us. I clenched my fists again, trying to hold back the sudden surge of panic that wanted to overtake me entirely. Every instinct I had screamed at me that we were out of our depth, miles from anything we knew. Maybe he would have been luckier if he hadn't woken up.

Marcus finally turned his head, his eyes landing on the wreckage scattered across the shoreline where we washed up. What was left of the boat barely resembled a vessel anymore—a couple jagged planks, a warped rib of the hull jutting up like a broken bone, and an oar twisted so badly it looked more like a large piece of driftwood than anything resembling a paddle. "Woah…"

I forced myself to take a deep breath, drawing the air into my lungs and holding it there until it ached. I needed something to anchor me, something steady when everything around me felt ripped apart. My hands were still shaking, my chest burning from the panic that had dragged me under and tossed me around during the storm. But I couldn't let myself spiral. Not here. Not now. The storm had passed, the boat was gone, but we were still alive. That had to matter more than the wreckage around us.

"Would you look at that…" Marcus eventually stood and brushed the wet sand from his arms, grinning like this was nothing more than a minor inconvenience. He had that infuriating look again, the one that made it clear he thought I was overreacting. "What's wrong? Can't handle a little hiccup?"

I whipped my head toward him, blinking in disbelief. My chest tightened with frustration, and the words flew out before I could temper them. "This isn't a hiccup! This is a disaster!" I pointed a finger toward the broken remains, my voice carrying harsher than I meant it to be. How could he look at the ruins of the only thing tethering us back to safety and call it a hiccup?

My gaze drifted upward toward the towering island behind us. The tree line rose like a wall, thick with green that seemed to pulse with a life of its own. Palms swayed gently at the edges, but deeper in, the vegetation tangled into knots of shadow that swallowed the light. I let my eyes roam past the trees, up and up until they caught on the massive mountain piercing the clouds. It stood far away, like some silent watcher, the peak sharp against the sky.

Something in my chest dropped as the realization sank in. I took a slow breath, lifted my hand, and pointed toward it. "We're still on the island. We're just on the other side! The village is just at the base of the mountain. It's only… several dozens of miles away…"

The words came out heavier than I expected. Saying them made the truth settle like a stone in my stomach. The distance stretched between us and the village, the miles of jungle, tangled paths, and whatever else the island had waiting. My throat tightened, and I lowered my hand, wishing I hadn't been the one to give shape to the fear that had been building in the back of my mind.

Marcus tilted his head toward the distant mountain, his grin widening as if the storm had been a minor inconvenience rather than a near-disaster. "So all we have to do is make it to that mountain? Piece of cake!" His confidence was almost infuriating.

He bounced on the balls of his feet, letting the sand squish between his toes, completely ignoring the wreckage of the boat at our feet. "You know," he added casually, "I love hiking. It's one of my favorite hobbies. This'll be nothing. We'll be back to the village in no time." His words were light, but my stomach knotted tighter with every syllable he spoke. "Also, I think you dropped these," he said, handing me my glasses that I had been desperately trying to find so I could see clearly.

I felt a cold weight settle in my chest. Nothing about this was going to be easy. The wind whipping off the water was sharp, but it didn't compare to the pressure in my mind. "It's not that simple," I said, my voice firmer than I intended. I brushed the sand stubbornly sticking to my arms and legs, trying to shake off the storm's aftermath.

The jungle between us and the mountain seemed endless, a giant mass of greens that made it impossible to estimate the true distance. I pointed toward it, trying to make him understand. "If I had to guess, the village is just under a two-day trip from here… if we're lucky." My words felt hollow even as I said them, but I couldn't ignore the reality pressing down on me. "And we haven't had too much luck." The thought of traversing the rough jungle terrain made my stomach churn: a day and a half of hiking, with no guarantee we'd even reach the village safely.

"Well how do we keep ourselves on track? What if we get there and the plane is gone? Or even worse, we get there and have to watch it as it's flying across the sky." Marcus said, chuckling.

One of his words stuck with me. Watch. "Marcus, that's it! My wrist watch!" I tapped at the small digital watch on my arm. It was dusted with sand and a little hard to read under the harsh sunlight, but it was working nonetheless. "This is our countdown!"

"A wrist watch?" Marcus smirked, "What's that gonna do, tell us what time it is when we make it back?"

"No! The watch has a twenty-four-hour countdown system, I've been using it each day since Victor told me about that plane coming," I explained, proud of myself for the idea. "When the countdown ends, I reset it for another day. We know we have to make it back in about 3 resets, so as long as we stay on course, this is our ticket back!"

"Hm… Not bad, Noah. Not bad at all."

I pointed my finger toward the mountain again, more for emphasis than anything else. "We *need* to make it back in those three days. I have a plane to catch, and I need to get off this stupid island." My chest tightened, my hands trembling slightly as I gestured. Fear and frustration surged up my throat, making my words catch at the edges. Every heartbeat felt like a reminder that neither time nor luck was on our side.

Marcus tilted his head, smiling like my panic was amusing, and I could feel the tension in my shoulders spike. My eyes scanned the jungle again, imagining the worst: jagged rocks hidden beneath moss, thick vines ready to twist around ankles and legs, insects too big to be real, and a whole list of dangerous animals lurking behind every shadow. Three days didn't feel like a generous estimate anymore—it felt like a ticking clock counting down to disaster.

I ran my hands down my face and exhaled sharply, trying to rein in the surge of my anxiety. "We really don't have time to mess around. Every second counts," I declared.

Marcus just chuckled, shaking his head like he had all the time in the world, and I clenched my fists, trying to ground myself. The pressure of the looming mountain, the endless jungle around us, and the ticking clock in my mind made me feel cornered. I couldn't let my nerves take over—not when every second could make the difference between making it to the village and being stuck here indefinitely. My gaze flicked back to the jagged peak in the distance, my chest tightening again. The thought of failing to reach the plane gnawed at me, and I couldn't let it. I had to make it. I had to push through.

Marcus grinned at me, kicking a bit of sand over his shoulder. "So we've got three days to make it back? Not bad. I like those odds." The casual way he said it made my stomach twist tighter. Three days felt impossible to me, especially with the way the jungle pressed in around us like it wanted to swallow every last trace of civilization. But to Marcus, three days was nothing, apparently.

All I could do was let out a long, exasperated sigh. "Well, I don't," I admitted, glaring at him more out of habit than actual anger. "We've got no food, no water, and no supplies to get us through this jungle! We'll be lucky if we don't get lost out here…" My words trailed off, but the tension in my chest didn't. I could already feel the heat from the sun and the nagging fear of being found a couple weeks from now dead in the jungle. "Who am I kidding? Without a guide of some kind, finding our way out in time is utterly hopeless…"

"Wait a second…" Marcus's eyes lit up as he began to dig in his back pocket. I blinked in disbelief as he pulled out a small golden compass and held it above him like it was some sort of treasure. "Aha!" he said, holding it up like he had just discovered the solution to every problem in the world.

I couldn't help the smile that tugged at my lips. Relief mingled with amusement, and I let out a short laugh. "Marcus! A compass! Way to pull through!" I said, feeling a spark of hope crack through the panic I'd been carrying since waking. By some miracle, the water hadn't stolen the compass from us. It was small, but it was enough to give me a foothold through all this chaos.

"Let me see once," I said as we bent over the compass together, and I pointed in the direction I'd been thinking all along. "The village… It's southeast from here. About 150 degrees to be precise," I said, tracing the line with my finger.

Marcus nodded, spinning the compass carefully and letting the needle settle before grinning like he had just unlocked a secret map.

"Now remember," he started, tapping the compass thoughtfully before leaning back and launching into a mini-lecture about hiking etiquette and jungle navigation, rattling off tips I didn't even realize I was absorbing. "Always keep your steps measured, look for natural water sources like waterfalls and fresh springs, always keep the sun at your back if you can—it can help you keep your bearings. And don't underestimate the undergrowth, it'll slow you down if you're not careful enough."

I stayed quiet, just listening, and I couldn't help but feel impressed. The way he explained everything made it sound almost easy, like he had done it a thousand times. I nodded along as he spoke even though the anxiety clawing at my chest refused to loosen. The compass in his hand, the clear direction, and the steady confidence Marcus carried, it was almost contagious. For a moment, I let myself believe that maybe we actually had a chance.

I glanced down at the compass. "Looks like we've got a good start now!" I said, trying to let some of my nervous energy spill into excitement instead. The sun hung high, glaring down through breaks in the canopy, which meant we needed to move if we wanted to stay on course. For the first time, I actually smiled at Marcus and held a hand out toward the jungle, as if I was presenting it to him. "Guessing the day's just getting started… Shall we?"

Marcus tucked the compass back into his pocket, his big grin still in place. "I'd say we shall! Let's do this," he said, sounding almost casual.

I nodded, letting another small smile creep onto my face. "Let's do this," I said. Something about his confidence—it was infectious. For the first time since I'd met him, I actually believed he could handle this, and that maybe, together, we could make it back in time.

We brushed the last of the sand off our clothes, shaking out sleeves and pant legs the best we could. The jungle ahead looked dense and green, but the compass in Marcus's pocket and the faint idea of what direction we should be in gave me a focus I hadn't had since we'd woken up in the sand.

As we started toward the trees, I noticed a rhythm forming between us, the kind that only comes when two people are in peril. More than a rhythm, maybe even a bond. The fear of being lost didn't disappear, but it felt more manageable now, pinned down beneath a layer of cautious optimism. The jungle was wild and intimidating, but somehow it felt less like a prison and more like the first stretch of the path home. Being stranded was awful, but maybe it wouldn't be so bad with someone else here.

Chapter Nine

The vegetation was thick, overwhelming, and humid. With no real path to follow, we relied on luck (and Marcus's lucky compass) to guide our way through. Branches scraped at my arms and legs as I pushed through the plantlife, leaves wet with dew drenching my clothes and hair. The smell of the air made everything around us feel so alive, so full of earth and growth, with the faint sweetness of flowers I couldn't name.

All around us were the sounds of the jungle: the crunch of broken twigs under our feet, the cawing and cooing of birds, and the faint rustle of hidden creatures through the underbrush. I kept half-expecting something to jump out at us, but it never did. If only I could be so lucky.

Marcus moved ahead of me so confidently, weaving through the dense vegetation with a kind of ease I envied. He didn't hesitate, didn't look back, just followed some invisible thread in his mind. I admired the way he adjusted his footing. He sidestepped low-hanging vines, and ducked under sharp, dead branches without a pause. It was like watching a creature that had always belonged here out for a stroll, while I was just a clumsy guest in its territory.

The sunlight filtered through the canopy in fragmented shards. It lit patches of the forest floor like spotlights, illuminating the many vibrant greens of the moss and ferns. Each shade seemed more vivid than the last. Bright lime clung to new leaves, while darker emeralds hid in shadowed recesses, and pastel patches of moss softened the jagged edges of broken branches. Occasionally, a flower bloomed a beautiful purple or pink, bursting against the monotony of green, each one perfectly preserved around us.

By now, we'd been hiking for over an hour, maybe two, and my muscles were beginning to protest worse than when I'd first woken up in the sand. I was beyond stiff from twisting around fallen logs and ducking under the low-hanging branches. Sweat mixed with the dew that ran down my back, soaking my shirt, and dripped into my eyes, stinging and blurring my vision for a moment. I shook my head, trying to clear it, and noticed Marcus moving ahead without any sign of fatigue. He paused sometimes, scanning the jungle, and I realized he wasn't just walking—he was reading it, following a set of rules I could only guess at, picking safe footing and spots where the vines were less tangled.

I could hear the tiny details of the ecosystem; the *drip, drip, drip* of water droplets falling from one leaf to another, the *buzz, buzz, buzz* of insects in the underbrush, the distant groan of wood bending under some unseen animal's weight. Each sound revealed a new detail as I looked around—a twisted root, a fern curled perfectly at the tip, a vine that hung in a perfect arc, ready to brush my face. I tried to memorize it all, though I knew it would be impossible.

The quiet rhythm of our footsteps and the hum of the jungle around us was interrupted by a sudden roar from my stomach. I stopped mid-step and pressed a hand against my belly, embarrassed. "I'm thinking it's lunchtime."

"I hear ya," Marcus said, rubbing his own stomach and giving me a sheepish grin. "I would give just about anything for a burger right now. A big one, double cheese, extra pickles."

I laughed despite myself, the sound mingling with the distant chatter of birds. "We're in the middle of a jungle, Marcus. I didn't think the nearest drive-thru was within walking distance. Not that a burger doesn't sound perfect right now, and the extra pickles only sweeten the thought," I said. "But cheese? Disgusting!"

"You don't put cheese on your burger?! You're crazy!" He shook his head, staring off into the dense foliage with a mix of frustration and longing. "But even without cheese, I would destroy a burger right now. Fries too. And a shake."

I couldn't help but grin at him. "That does sound delicious," I admitted, imagining sinking my teeth into a juicy, salty burger. The nice refreshing pickles, the savory smashed patties, and the soft bun barely holding it all together. My stomach growled again, louder this time, making me wince.

We paused, standing among the towering trees, the damp leaves brushing against our arms, and surveyed our surroundings. Everywhere we looked, it was nothing but endless green—trunks twisting up into the canopy, vines curling across branches, ferns spreading across the forest floor. There wasn't a sign of anything resembling food within reach.

I tilted my head, scanning the upper branches, and noticed large clusters of fruit hanging high above us. Bright oranges and reds, small and almost teasingly out of reach. "Well…" I started, rubbing my stomach, "unless one of those trees grows hamburgers, we might have to settle for the fruit."

Marcus followed my gaze and let out a long sigh. "Yeah… I guess that's our only option. But look at them," he said, gesturing toward the towering branches, "They're way too high up there. How are we supposed to get any?"

I rubbed my chin, trying to think. The jungle looked unforgiving, the branches high and twisted, the trunks thick and menacing. Yet the thought of starving made the fruit suddenly seem like the most precious treasure in the world. Each piece looked plump, sun-drenched in the rays of light that filtered through the canopy.

We both stood there quietly, staring up at the fruit, my stomach protesting again. Marcus kicked at a low-hanging branch in frustration. "I'd climb it if I could, but… look at that," he said, gesturing at the rough, slick bark and the empty spaces between sturdy branches. "There's no way I'd make it."

I nodded, feeling the hunger gnawing at me. I glanced at Marcus, who seemed equally torn between patience and the impulse to go for it, and I realized we were both thinking the same thing: hunger made even the impossible feel like a challenge worth trying.

Suddenly, Marcus stopped and crouched down, his hand darting toward the ground. "Here we go!" he exclaimed, eyes lighting up. I instinctively leaned closer, curious despite myself, trying to figure out what had caught his attention in the thick undergrowth.

I watched in disgust as he grabbed a shriveled, dried-up papaya half-buried in the dirt.

"You're seriously going to eat that?" I asked, wrinkling my nose. The thing looked like it had been rotting for weeks—its skin wrinkled, tough, and almost black in places, like a relic left behind by some past season. "That's revolting."

"Ew, no." Marcus gave me a disgusted look, like I was insane for thinking he was going to eat it. He held it out like a grenade. "Don't be ridiculous. I have better ideas."

He turned the shriveled papaya over in his hands, tapping it lightly on the ground as if preparing it for a bigger plan. Then, without any warning, he swung his arm and flung it upward. My eyes followed the arc before I heard a sharp *thunk* as it hit the branches above. A soft rustle answered it, then the dull thump of several fresh papayas hitting the forest floor.

I blinked, trying to process what just happened. There, scattered around the base of the tree, lay four ripe, plump papayas. Their orange-yellow skin glinted delectably in the light. My stomach growled once again at the sight, and all I could manage was a stunned, "Oh… smart."

Marcus grinned at me, clearly proud of his work. "See?" he said, brushing dirt off his hands. "Knowledge of the great outdoors, Noah. That's all you need out here."

I shook my head, staring at the fallen papayas, trying to process both the sheer luck and the cleverness of it. Marcus had this way of taking what seemed hopeless—a shriveled fruit nobody would touch—and turning it into a tool. I didn't know if it was instinct, luck, or just pure audacity, but every time he did something like this, I felt a combination of admiration and disbelief.

Marcus crouched and picked up one of the papayas, turning it over in his hands. "I'll admit, I didn't think it would be that easy," he said. "This is… perfect." He held it out toward me, a half-smile on his face.

"You're insane," I said, finally breaking my gaze from the fruit and looking at him, shaking my head with amusement and admiration. "But… you're also kind of brilliant."

Marcus chuckled, clearly enjoying the praise I'd just given him. "Thanks."

"No problem!" My stomach growled again, louder this time. Marcus glanced at me, and I could see that familiar spark in his eyes, the same one that had led him to take this risk in the first place.

"You gonna grab one, or just look at them?" he asked, grinning.

I stepped closer, reaching down to grab one, feeling the weight of it in my hands.

The two of us sank down onto the damp forest floor, the fallen papayas scattered between us like the feast that it was. Marcus grabbed one of the fruits, peeling back the skin with a few quick, forceful motions before biting down with a satisfying crunch. Juice dripped down his chin almost immediately, and he didn't seem to care in the slightest, tearing into the flesh with reckless hunger.

Unlike Marcus, my bites were small and careful, chewing deliberately, wiping my mouth with the back of my hand after each one to avoid looking sloppy. The contrast between us was almost comical. I couldn't help sneaking glances at him while he ate, taking in the way his hands were sticky with juice and his expression softened with relief and satisfaction. The world around us seemed to fade for a moment, leaving just the two of us and this chaotic little meal. There was something undeniably cute in the way he demolished the fruit, how clearly he was enjoying it without concern for manners or appearances.

Marcus noticed my gaze and smirked, lifting a piece of papaya toward his mouth and biting again without pause. "You're staring," he said between mouthfuls, juice glinting in the sunlight. "Why are you eating so slow?"

I cleared my throat, looking down at the fruit in my hands and taking another measured bite. "I'm not," I said, though my voice carried less conviction than I would have liked. "Just taking sensible bites."

"Uh-huh," he said, still chewing. "Sure." His smirk widened, and I felt heat creep into my cheeks. The messy way he ate, the sheer force with which he attacked the fruit—it was frustratingly attractive.

I tried to focus, to maintain some semblance of composure, but it was impossible not to watch him, to notice how the juice dripped onto his fingers and how he barely noticed. The hunger in him was so raw, so honest, and it made the jungle around us feel both more dangerous and more intimate at the same time.

Despite my attempts to dismiss it, the image stuck in my mind. He wasn't my type, and I had to remind myself of that repeatedly. Still, there was something in the way he devoured the papayas that made me think, fleetingly, that maybe if he were…different, things could be easier. Instead of being alone together, we could be *alone* together.

We sat there in the shade, eating the last of our fruit. Marcus leaned back against the trunk of a tree, wiping his sticky fingers on his pants, though most of the juice still clung stubbornly. He chewed another bite of papaya before speaking, eyes narrowing with curiosity. "So tell me, Teachy, why do you wanna leave this place so bad? We've only been here a couple days. And it's beautiful here!"

I laughed softly, brushing a strand of hair from my forehead. "Teachy, huh? And yeah it is beautiful. I don't think anybody could deny that.

But, well, I guess I'm just… out of my element." I took the last bite of papaya before continuing, "I've spent the last couple years in classrooms, learning to build a structured environment. And now, I don't have that. I have to start from the ground up, and I'm just not ready." My words felt awkward in the air, like they didn't quite reach the point I wanted to make, but Marcus didn't seem to mind.

"Not ready? Or not ready to let yourself be ready?" he asked, chewing half a papaya in his mouth, juice dripping from the corners of his lips like he didn't notice.

I blinked at him, taken aback. "That doesn't make sense."

He smirked, tilting his head. "Sure it does. You've been at school, working hard for that degree and everything. You always had a plan or someone telling you what to do. You always knew what was coming next. But here, you're the one who makes the plan. You've got no idea what's coming next. You're on your own and you're scared. Even though we both know you're more than capable of doing it."

I shifted uncomfortably, trying to digest more than just the fruit. The weight of his words settled differently than anything I've ever heard in the classroom. But maybe he was right. In school, the path had always been mapped out for me step by step, with clear instructions in bold print. Here, every choice was mine, and for once, there wasn't a syllabus or lecture notes to follow. The realization made my fingers tingle with both excitement and dread, and I chewed thoughtfully on the last bite of papaya, letting Marcus' words linger.

Then I realized, Marcus wasn't just spouting random thoughts or trying to impress me with his crazy jungle survival skills; there was an actual depth. There was more to this guy than I originally thought. A momentary flicker of surprise crossed my face, one I couldn't hide even if I wanted to. He leaned forward, resting his elbows on his knees, his messy, hungry grin softened.

"Alright, alright, big thinker," I said, a smirk tugging at my lips despite myself. "You heard half of my story at the airport and think you got me figured out? What about you? What's your story?"

Marcus finally put the last bite of fruit in his mouth before bringing a finger up and sucking the juice off. I felt my face heat up again. A sudden, undeniable blush creeping across my cheeks. I looked down, pretending to inspect the ground, but I couldn't ignore the way my stomach flipped at the careless, almost primal way he cleaned himself. It was the kind of thing that made me simultaneously annoyed at my own reaction and slightly amused.

He stretched his arms above his head, eyes half-closed, a faint smirk playing on his lips. "Nothing too interesting," he said finally. "I went to

Catholic school when I was younger, got really involved in the church, and eventually I became a missionary."

I blinked, trying to process how straightforward he was being. "That's all I get?" I asked, feeling a little frustrated despite the blush still covering my face. "Doesn't really seem fair, I shared a lot more with you. How about where you went to college? Where are you from? Did you always want to be a missionary?"

"Sorry," he shrugged, the kind of casual shrug that somehow made it clear he wasn't about to spill everything, but he'd given me a glimpse. I studied him, noting the lines in his face, the easy confidence, and the quiet intensity behind those dark eyes. There was more beneath the surface, I could feel it. "I only like to talk about the important stuff, I guess."

The sun shifted, casting a warm glow over the papaya-strewn ground, and I realized just how messy and human this moment felt. Marcus was right in front of me, unapologetically himself, and I had to admit it was kind of impressive, even if he was infuriatingly blunt. I shook my head, trying to hide my thoughts, but the urge to know more about him was gnawing at the back of my mind.

I tried to push down the weird mix of curiosity and something else I wasn't supposed to feel. "Come on," I said finally, forcing my voice to stay even. "You owe me more than that. Give me something real to work with. There has to be more between going to a religious school and ending up here."

"Maybe," Marcus said before letting out a short, almost nervous chuckle. "But I don't wanna get into it," he said, tossing the empty fruit rind to the side, the juice glinting in the sun for a brief second. "It's boring stuff."

"I didn't mean to pry, really. I was just wondering… you know, what made you choose the path you did?" I asked, wiping my face. "I mean, I know you're a missionary, but… I guess I just wondered if that was always your plan growing up, or if something happened that pushed you that way."

Marcus stopped mid-step for a moment, his face tightening. Then he glanced at me, a flicker of something unreadable in his eyes, before his finally jaw set. "Just drop it!" His voice was sharp, but underneath it I felt something tighter, more protective.

I felt the color leave my face, heat rising to my cheeks. "Sorry," I said quickly, keeping my tone low, almost pleading, like I hadn't intended to press too far. My chest felt tight, and I swallowed hard, trying to shake off the tension that appeared between us. "Let's keep going."

We started moving again, our boots pressing into the damp, leaf-strewn jungle floor. The only sounds that filled the air were our footsteps and the occasional call of animals in the distance. Somewhere far off a bird called out, its cry echoing against the trees. Crickets chirped from the ground below. Every step felt heavier, weighed down by the silence stretching between us.

I couldn't stop thinking about Marcus now, trying to figure out why the topic had hit such a nerve. Normally, I wasn't the type to care so much about someone else's private life, but the way he'd brushed me off gnawed at me. *Why did I care so much? Why did it feel like there was a wall I had to get past, even though he clearly didn't want me to?* And despite my best effort to push it away, the answer seemed as elusive as the sunlight flickering through the canopy: unreachable.

Chapter Ten

Marcus still didn't acknowledge me. Any time I tried to say something to him, he looked at me and said nothing. Sometimes, he doesn't even look at me. We hiked for a while, and I was looking around at the tall trees, the vines, and the bored chirping of birds in the branches. We had been together for several hours, and the sun was about to go down. We have been racing the clock every day, and we yet again will not get back to the village tonight.

Another few hours had passed, and the sky had suddenly filled with clouds that looked like they were about to pour down on us, again.

"Uh oh, looks like we should stop and find some shelter before we get soaked," I said to Marcus.

Marcus said nothing.

"Marcus–," I said, just before my stomach felt upset. I let out a groan in pain.

"Do you mind?" Marcus said to me, still not looking in my direction.

"Something is wrong," I pleaded in pain.

"Suck it up. You're fine."

"No, I don't feel good. I think I'm going to vomit." Just after finishing that sentence, it felt like gallons of salt water erupted from my esophagus and all over the jungle floor.

"Oh geez. Are you okay?" Marcus asked.

The rain started to pick up, and we knew we had to find a place to set up a shelter for the night. I watched as Marcus pointed toward a hollowed out treetrunk and said, "There! We can throw some thick canopy leaves over the holes and make a shelter for the night."

I looked up, still crouched to the ground, not sure if I would be able to walk.

I tried to get up, but I wasn't able to.

"Come on, kid. You go this," Marcus said.

I tried, but I failed once again.

Marcus looked around, trying to figure out what to do, before walking over to me with his arms out. To my surprise, Marcus picked me up and cradled me to the tree trunk. I was surprised at how strong Marcus was. I never expected him to do something like that for me.

Marcus carried me over to the tree trunk and placed me down on some dry ground, which was just a section of moss.

"Thank you," I said to him, just before letting out a sour cough.

"Don't mention it," he replied.

"I don't feel good at all." I shifted to my stomach, trying to find a position that felt comfortable to lay in.

"You threw up a lot, and you haven't had any fresh water since we left the hut. We could both use some water."

"If we want water we–"

"We'd need a filter. We obviously don't have that. And, we haven't passed any streams yet." Marcus looked around and a couple dozen yards away, he spotted a coconut tree. "Bingo! Coconut water will be more than hydrating!"

I was annoyed that Marcus cut me off in the middle of my sentence, but I was happy to see he was showing efforts to take care of us until we could get back to the village. Marcus was more intelligent than I anticipated, especially in events like this.

Marcus walked toward a coconut tree before removing his denim jacket and using it to help him climb to the top. As Marcus hit the coconuts, causing them to fall to the ground, I realized that I was crushing on Marcus. Even though he was a jerk, he carried me to the tree trunk to get me out of the rain, and he helped to get some fruit and water.

Did I really like Marcus? Was I just feeling lonely? Does Marcus even like me?

All of these questions started running through my mind.

Marcus returned to the shelter with two coconuts in his hands. He is soaked from the rain. His curls were dripping water as if he was in the shower. Since he removed his jacket to help him climb the tree, his white tank top had become see-through from the water. It revealed his beautifully sculpted body underneath.

As Marcus prepared the coconuts for us to drink, I kept staring at him.

I do like him. I hope he likes me, too.

The coconuts were enough to rehydrate both Marcus and me, and we had made sufficient progress to return to the village.

As the rain continued to fill the sound barrier, we finished our coconuts and both began to feel more alive. I was still laying on the moss, and Marcus was still very quiet. He was leaned up against the inner wall of the tree trunk.

I sat up a bit and said, "Thank you for carrying me here, finding me water, and something to eat earlier."

Marcus replied with a quiet, "Mhm."

"I'm sorry about earlier, Marcus. I didn't mean to pry." Marcus stayed quiet. The only sound was the rain drops hitting the leaves on the ground.

After a few more moments of silence, I spoke up, again. "Neither of us want to be stuck out here, Marcus. I know you're mad at me. I just want us to try and make the best of it together."

"I'm not mad at you, Noah," Marcus responded. I sat there, waiting for more. "It's just...complicated," he added.

"Well, if you decide you want to talk about it, I'll listen. Even though you barely remembered when I told you my story."

Marcus smirked and said, "Back at the airport? I heard you. You graduated top of your class. You were nervous about the first teaching job. You never left California before. I got it all, I just played it cool."

"You're a jerk." I scolded him.

Marcus laughed and said, "My bad. What am I supposed to say?"

"How about: 'I'm sorry.' I poured my heart out to you!"

"Alright, alright. You want my story? Here is my story."

I sat up and listened to Marcus's story.

"I was born and raised in Westerly, Rhode Island. It was a very nice town, full of people that have no idea what to do with all of their money. I lived in an oversized house along the ocean with my mom, my dad, and my twin brother. The house was so big that it was where all of my family would come to celebrate the holidays. I was never big into school, so when I graduated high school, I decided not to go to college. It just wasn't for me. I wanted to find something I had always wanted to do."

"So what did you do?" I asked.

"I got super involved in the church. My family had always had a heavy religious presence, so they wanted me to do the same. I volunteered and helped out. After a while, I felt stuck in a rut and saw an opportunity to become a missionary in Fiji, so I decided that I wanted to change the world. My family wasn't supportive of my choices. They loved me, but didn't love the choices I made sometimes."

As he spoke, I saw a tear forming in his eyes. For the guy that seemed so confident all the time, it was weird to see him be vulnerable, even a little.

"I guess that's normal, right? I packed up my life and left my family behind and never looked back. It was hard, and I knew that I might never be able to come back, but I had to do what my heart told me was right."

I didn't know what to say. I didn't know this was what led him to being here, so I said, "Marcus, I'm so sorry. I know how hard it is to leave your family behind for your calling. You're so much stronger than I am. I know my limits, and I can't stay on this island like you. I miss my family way too much."

"Yeah. It is what it is," Marcus said in a sad tone.

"I appreciate you telling me, but I think it is my bedtime."

Marcus looked over and said, "What do you mean, it's only…5:37 p.m.? I think my watch is broken."

I laughed and then turned onto my side. I lay on the moss, using my sweater as a pillow.

"Goodnight, Marcus," I said.

"Night, Noah," he replied. "Sleep well."

Chapter Eleven

My eyelids felt like they'd been weighed down by sandbags, hesitant to open no matter how hard I tried. A haze clung to my vision, light filtering in through the slats of the shelter in soft, uneven streaks. My body was stiff, every muscle still half-asleep, the remnants of my dreams tugging at me to stay under just a little longer. I looked over to Marcus but was met with nothing. The corner where Marcus had been the night before was now empty, like he had never been there at all. I was alone.

For a moment, a nervous pang struck me—the quiet pressed in heavier when he wasn't there. For the first moment since we got here, I had some time to myself. It was freeing, almost like I was home again. But beneath that, something else rose up, something that had been simmering for days. It was like the stillness gave me permission. I pulled up my shirt, exposing my chest, and undid my pants in one swift motion. My mind began racing to unholy places.

My body felt restless. Heat rushed through my chest, pooling lower until I couldn't ignore it anymore. The only relief from this feeling was to stroke it out. My muscles tightened, then relaxed as I gave in to the pull. I shut my eyes and let images of Marcus fill the space in my head—his grin, the way his shoulders flexed when he carried supplies, the sweat that glistened across his arms when the sun hit him just right. Every detail only heightened the ache building inside me, feeding into the pleasure.

Breath hitched, shoulders tense, I let myself move with the rhythm of that wanting. My skin felt too warm, damp even, and I had to bite down on my lip to keep quiet, like the forest might overhear me. A soft moan escaped from me. The air felt thick, hot, wrapping around me until I couldn't tell if the pounding in my ears was my pulse or from the thoughts of him.

Release finally tore through me. My discharge spilled forward, hot and sudden, spreading across my abdomen and chest. My whole body seized in a rush of ecstasy, shuddering as the sensation pulsed out in waves. One rope after another. It felt endless, every second dragging me further, until I collapsed back against my mossy resting place, my chest heaving.

I stayed there, catching my breath, hand slick with my juices, body humming with the aftershocks. My head spun, equal parts relief and guilt twisting inside me. I had let myself imagine him too vividly, too completely. It was wrong, but it felt so right. I was no longer crushing on Marcus, I was obsessed.

When it was over, I sank back against the ground, chest heaving, sweat and my own juices clinging to me. My body hummed with relief and joy and with thoughts of Marcus. Always Marcus. As I sat there in my own mess, I imagined for a moment Marcus right there with me: the two of us making our own mess together.

I wiped my face with my arm, trying to compose myself, though the heat in my cheeks wouldn't go away. I knew I had to move; Marcus was somewhere nearby, and if I lingered too long I might expose too much. I quickly buttoned my pants and ran my fingers through my sweaty hair, trying to look as though I hadn't just pleasured myself.

I pushed myself up slowly, the rough ground beneath me shifting as I sat up fully. My back popped, a small relief against the stiffness lingering in my body. The air was cool now against my skin, carrying traces of damp earth and leaves. The trunk of the tree creaked softly above me, branches settling, as though acknowledging my unholy movements.

I rubbed at my eyes with the heels of my palms, the grit of sleep wiped away as I pressed harder than I needed to. A yawn forced its way out, my jaw cracking as I stretched it wide. My hands fell to my lap, fingers twitching with the restless urge to move, to do something. But for a moment I just sat there, caught in the strangeness of what just transpired.

I walked toward the doorway, ducking under the low opening of the tree and stepping outside, the morning air damp against my skin. The forest seemed louder now that I was outside—birds cawing from somewhere high in the canopy, insects buzzing in a chaotic rhythm, the small trickles of dew filling the space around me.

"Marcus?" My voice cracked, softer than I meant it to be. I cleared my throat and tried again, louder this time. "Marcus! Where are you?"

For a moment, only the forest answered me back, and my stomach clenched with unease. Then, faintly, a reply carried through the trees: "I'm over here!"

I pushed forward through the brush, my steps crunching over damp leaves as I followed the sound. Branches tugged at my shirt as I continued to shove through the patch of brush, the smell of smoke growing stronger the closer I got. When I finally broke into a small clearing, I spotted him.

Marcus was at the edge of the clearing, crouched by a stream. A modest fire crackled in the center of it all. Over the fire, two large fish had been skewered on green sticks, their skin blistering and crisping as the flames worked their magic. A faint hiss rose each time the juices dripped into the fire, sending up a curl of smoky steam that made my stomach tighten with hunger.

Beside him, he'd arranged a surprisingly neat collection of food. A cluster of round, golden fruits rested in a small pile. Next to them was a scatter of small, reddish nuts cracked open to reveal their pale insides, their shells stacked carefully to the side. A few green leaves, flat and broad, had been laid out almost like plates, holding pieces of fruit that Marcus had already sliced with what I can only imagine was a sharp rock. The colors of the buffet looked almost vibrant against the dark soil and green trees, yellows and reds popping out like a portrait painted onto the ground.

"Woah…" It was truly nothing I'd ordinarily give a second thought, but after all we'd been through, this looked like something out of a dream. My stomach growled so loudly I thought Marcus might hear it over the fire.

"Impressed?" Marcus's shirt clung to him, damp with sweat that shimmered along his shoulders and arms in the glow of the fire. His hair was wild and uneven, like he'd pushed it back with his hands a dozen times while working. Even his jaw looked sharper in the early light, tight with focus as he leaned over the flames to turn the fish.

"Uh, yeah!" A laugh slipped out, more a nervous giggle than anything else. "What's all this?" I asked, gesturing toward the fire, the neat pile of fruits and nuts, and the fish sizzling on their makeshift skewers. "I could have helped you, ya know."

Marcus glanced up, his smile easy, like he'd been waiting for me to see. "Well, you looked so comfortable, and I woke up pretty early, so I figured I'd make us some breakfast."

"Thanks, Marcus," I felt my face warm and rubbed the back of my neck, trying to play it off. "That's so kind of you!" I said, full of admiration.

He shrugged, tossing a stick into the fire and watching the sparks jump. "It was nothing really. Just trying to make myself useful!"

I raised an eyebrow, teasing him. "I didn't know you could cook."

Marcus smirked, leaning back on his hands. "'Cook' is a strong word. More like scavenge. With style." He made a mock flourish with his hand toward the spread, like he was presenting some grand feast.

That broke something in me, and I laughed—really laughed. The kind that made my shoulders shake and left me catching my breath. Marcus laughed too and for a moment it felt like we weren't stranded or desperate or tired. We were just… us.

I leaned closer to the fire, letting the heat hit my face and the smell of roasted fish settle over me. "Well, style or not," I said, still smiling, "it looks pretty impressive from where I'm sitting."

He tilted his head, giving me a half-grin that made me look down at my hands before the flutter in my chest could get worse. Marcus used a larger stick to remove the fish from the fire and handed one to me, along with a small portion of berries and fruit. "Here you are. Eat up, Teachy."

"Thank you," I said, examining the meal before me. The fish was crisp on the outside, tender once I began to bite into it. The smoky flavor from the fire gave it something richer than I expected. My stomach practically sang with relief. I tried to pace myself, but each bite seemed to vanish too quickly, washed down with a handful of sweet, juicy fruit that stained my fingers.

Across from me, Marcus didn't hold back—he tore into his share with the same reckless hunger he always seemed to bring to everything, juice dripping down his chin, his fingers sticky once again with papaya. I couldn't help but glance at him now and then, caught somewhere between being impressed and a little amused by the sight.

"This is really good," I said between bites, my voice muffled by a mouthful of food. I hadn't expected to enjoy it this much, not when I'd been imagining another day of gnawing on unripe fruit or going hungry altogether.

Marcus chewed, swallowed, then looked at me curiously and said, "So, are we still on track?" His tone was casual, but I could see in his eyes he wanted reassurance.

I nodded, looking at my watch, setting down the half-eaten piece of fish in my hand. "Yeah, we are. But we've got to make sure we keep up the pace. If we slow down too much, three days could turn into four, maybe longer. In which case we'd be way too late for me to make that flight home."

"Well we can't have that." He grinned around another bite, tossing the stripped bones of a fish back toward the edge of the fire. "Then we better keep going, huh?"

I gave him a half-smile and popped the last piece of fruit into my mouth, savoring the sweetness as I licked the juice from my lips. "Guess we'd better."

The fire crackled between us, its smoke drifting lazily upward, and for a moment I wished we could sit there a while longer. How nice it would be for the two of us to enjoy this paradise together with no time limit holding us back. But the reminder of how far we still had to go pressed at the back of my mind. I dragged my sleeve across my face, wiping away the last traces of juice and sweat, and pushed myself upright, my legs still heavy from the meal.

"All set?" Marcus asked as he stood and dusted himself off, then turned to me with an easy grin, offering me his hand. His palm was open, waiting, steady in a way I hadn't expected. I slid my hand into his, and before I could brace myself, he pulled me up with a strength that surprised me. My body lurched forward, and suddenly, there wasn't any space between us.

We ended up face to face, almost nose to nose. His breath brushed against my skin, warm and quick. I froze. Every detail around me seemed to sharpen all of a sudden. I couldn't help but notice the faint shimmer of sweat clinging to his hairline, the curve of his smile that had faltered, the way his chest rose and fell faster than before. The world felt like it had narrowed down to just the two of us in that moment, the jungle sounds fading into the background. I had a feeling I'd be thinking of this moment again the next time I was alone.

I felt heat flooding my face, climbing from my neck all the way up to my ears. I tried to step back, but my feet didn't seem to move. I didn't think I wanted them to. My heart was pounding, wild and out of rhythm, and when I opened my mouth to speak, the words tumbled out, uneven and clumsy. "O-oh gosh! Look at the s-sun! We g-gotta go!" I blurted, my words tripping over themselves.

Marcus let out an awkward laugh, scratching the back of his neck with his free hand. His cheeks were tinged with color too, and for a split second, I wondered if he was as rattled as I was. "Yep! Good idea!" he said quickly.

As we started moving again, I couldn't shake the memory of his touch, the way his hand had felt so warm and sure when he'd lifted me. I missed him already, more than I wanted to admit, and I didn't even know if he felt the same. The thought of being near him, so close and so calm while I felt like a mess inside, made my head spin. I swallowed hard, trying to steady my racing heart, even though I knew I was too far gone.

Chapter Twelve

For the next couple of hours, Marcus and I followed a stream, the sound of rushing water growing stronger with every step. For a while, I'd thought it was just the water picking up speed along the bank, but pretty quickly the sound swelled into something deeper, like the earth itself had turned on its well. When the trees finally thinned, we saw it—a towering waterfall crashing down into a foamy pool. The mist rose like soft white curtains blanketing the air around us.

"Wow…" Marcus's face lit up the second he saw it. His eyes widened, and he grinned like a kid at a candy store. "Look's like it's time for a much-needed shower!" he said, spreading his arms out like he was presenting the sight before us.

Before I could even react, he shrugged his jacket off, draping it on a nearby rock. His movement was casual, confident even, but my chest tightened all the same. My cheeks burned hot at the sight of his broad shoulders, and I became very aware of the way my eyes were lingering longer than they should. The front section of my pants noticed, too. I tried to look anywhere else—at the mist of the water, the ripples racing across the pool, the frogs leaping from one lilypad to another—but no matter what, my gaze kept drifting back to him.

"How are we supposed to…you know…" The words stumbled out of my mouth. "We don't really have towels or anything." My voice cracked a little, betraying the fact that my thoughts were running miles ahead of my own comfort zone. "I don't know if we should—"

"Worried about me seeing your weiner?" Marcus threw his head back and laughed, his shoulders shaking with it. The sound bounced off the cliff walls surrounding the waterfall. "We're both guys, Noah. I don't care if you don't."

The way he said it was so simple, like it wasn't a big deal at all, like the only thing here making it weird was me. He had such easy confidence that left me floundering, unsure if I should try and mirror it myself or just shrink away. My hands curled awkwardly at my sides, and I found myself shuffling one foot against the damp soil, pretending like I wasn't completely flustered.

The roar of the water made it hard to think clearly, but somehow my thoughts still found a way to tangle themselves up. I kept stealing glances at

Marcus as he tugged at his clothes, removing them layer by layer with a kind of careless ease that only made me more self-conscious.

"I mean…" My voice caught in my throat, and I forced myself to clear it. "It's not exactly private out here. I guess I don't care if *you* see me, but what if someone—"

Marcus shot me a look over his shoulder, that cocky grin tugging at his mouth. The mist blurred the sharpness of his features, but his expression was still clear enough. He wasn't worried. Not even close. "That's what makes it fun," he said, kicking his boots off so they landed with a thud on the wet ground. "And besides, we need a bath!"

He was right, of course. Days of sweat and dirt and musk clung to me, and the thought of rinsing it all away under the torrent of the water was tempting. But to undress in front of each other… let alone the fact that it was with the guy I was obsessed with.

"Come on, Noah," Marcus said, his tone lighter now, teasing but not unkind. "You can stand there blushing all day, or you can actually enjoy the water. Enjoy the view," he grinned.

My ears burned hotter than my cheeks, and I found myself staring at the ground, tracing the lines of mud between the roots. He made it sound so easy, but nothing about this felt easy to me. I wanted to, but I just couldn't make myself undress.

Marcus didn't waste another second. He hooked his thumbs under the hem of his tank top and peeled it up over his head. My breath snagged before I even realized it. My eyes dragged across every line of him that the fabric had been hiding. His chest caught the light, broad and strong, skin bronzed from the sun but streaked with dirt and sweat that only seemed to sharpen the way he looked. His abs were firm, cut so clearly I felt my throat tighten just looking at them. And the rest of him, his shoulders, his arms, everything, was like something carved out of marble. Even his chest, smooth and bare, caught me off guard in a way I couldn't shake.

The heat shot down through me so quickly it was almost a shock. I clenched my jaw, but that didn't stop the inevitable from happening. My body reacted before my brain could get a grip on itself, and I shifted on my feet, mortified at how obvious it felt in my pants.

Marcus must've caught the color blazing across my face as I looked at him, because he just grinned wide and chuckled. "Take a picture, it'll last longer."

My head snapped down, and I waved my hands in front of me like that could erase the whole moment. "Sorry, sorry!" My words tumbled.

He just laughed harder, shaking his head like the whole thing was harmless fun, like he had no idea what he was doing to me. Or maybe he did, and he just didn't care.

I wanted this. I wanted him, and I couldn't stand still any longer. I stumbled toward a patch of bushes at the edge of the clearing and began to undress. My heart hammered in my chest, every beat reminding me how close I'd come to completely losing my composure in front of him. My hands trembled as I started tugging at my shirt, my pants, every layer sticking to my skin. The air felt cooler, naked, shaded and damp, but my body still burned.

Even as I stood there in my birthday suit, I couldn't keep my curiosity in check. My eyes drifted back through the branches, trying to sneak a peek at him without my permission. He was still by the water, his movements slow, confident in the way he carried himself. My breath caught again when I saw him reach for the waistband of his pants, the muscles in his back shifting. I told myself to look away, to focus on my own undressing, but I couldn't help it—I kept peeking, each glimpse sending another jolt through me.

I knew I should've looked away. I told myself over and over not to stare, that I was invading a moment he hadn't invited me into. My chest felt tight, my stomach twisting in ways that had nothing to do with hunger or exhaustion. But the second his pants slid down, my eyes betrayed me.

Marcus stepped free of the fabric of his boxers and shorts and stood there for a moment, the mist drifting around him from the waterfall, droplets clinging to his skin and shimmering in the sun. I could hear my own pulse thumping in my ears. He was—God, he was impeccable. His butt was round and firm, every curve and line defined like it had been sculpted with hours of dedication. His legs were thick and strong, the kind that could carry him anywhere, through any jungle or across any mountain. The dark hair dusting them caught the light in a way that made my brain short-circuit. Even his calves flexed and relaxed with each subtle movement.

Then my gaze drifted higher, and my heart felt like it'd stopped. I wasn't prepared for the beautiful sight of his chest, legs, and abdomen, but the rest of him was even better. He was clean shaven, tanned, and big. Bigger than I would have expected. I was frozen, heart hammering so loudly I was sure he could hear it. My brain was screaming at me to look away, to give him privacy, but my body refused to comply.

I fumbled with my own pile of clothes, and in an effort to conceal myself, grabbed a leaf off the ground that could barely cover my own pelvic area.

The leaf in my hand was ridiculous, thin and fragile, but it was all I could do to cover myself. My fingers gripped it tightly as I stepped out of the bushes, every step toward the water feeling like walking on a tightrope. My heart was a drum, my cheeks burned, and the knot in my stomach only tightened the closer I got.

The sound of the falls filled the air, masking my ragged breathing. Marcus was now in the pool, half-floating near the edge, his hair plastered to his forehead, droplets of water rolling down the slope of his shoulders and chest. He leaned back, arms stretched along the surface, completely at ease, as if he belonged in this moment here more than anywhere else.

I forced myself to move closer to him, careful to keep the leaf in place, my feet sinking into the soft sand at the water's edge. Every step gave me a new angle of him. The water itself was mesmerizing, rippling gently as it clung to him and pulled at the reflections of sunlight. Maybe it was just him that made the water so mesmerizing.

Marcus shifted, catching a glimpse of me stepping forward, and laughed, a warm sound that sent another jolt through me. My ears burned, my face hot, and I hugged the leaf tighter to my privates, wondering if I looked as ridiculous as I felt, although I already knew I did. I could see the faint mist of water on his skin, droplets glinting along the curve of his shoulders, tracing the line of his chest. Even relaxed, he radiated energy, strength, and something that made it impossible for me to look anywhere else.

I let out a shaky breath, forcing my legs to move closer to the pool, keeping the leaf pressed firmly against me, wishing so bad I had picked a larger one. I looked down at myself for the first time since grabbing the leaf and noticed the only thing it covered was half of my member and the upper portion of my balls. Everything else was a sight for him (or anyone else) to behold.

Marcus grinned when he saw me. "Come on in, Teachy, the water's fine," he called, his voice carrying over the steady roar of the falls.

I swallowed hard, "A-a-alright. I-I'm c-coming," I stammered, my words sounding absurd even to me. My heart was hammering in my chest and my palms were sweaty as I clutched my leaf tightly, pressing it firmly in front of my now growing erection.

Each step in the shallow edge of the water's bank sent a shiver through me. The water was cool at my ankles at first, then creeping up over my knees, sending a chill that contrasted with the warmth of the sun overhead. I kept my eyes fixed on the leaf in my hands, careful not to look at Marcus directly, even though every part of me wanted to.

I kept taking slow steps, the water reaching my thighs now. My hands gripped the leaf tighter, the pressure in my chest rising as I realized my erection was impossible to hide completely. I prayed Marcus wasn't looking at me, or worse, noticing, and tried to focus on the water swirling around me.

The way Marcus moved in the pool only made it harder to focus. Every shift of his body showed more of his athletic form. It was amazing: the tightness of his stomach, the definition of his abs, and the bulky strength in his legs as they pressed against the water. The sun reflected off the droplets of his chest, creating tiny sparks along the contours of his muscles, and my brain was in awe.

I took a breath and allowed the water to rise to my waist, the cool liquid brushing against my skin and dampening the sticky sweat from the jungle. I kept the leaf in place, pressing it as close to me as I could, moving cautiously closer while keeping my gaze down as I brought my whole body into the water. Keeping everything below my neck submerged.

After a moment of soaking there, we edged closer to the waterfall, ready for a shower. Marcus didn't hesitate. He stepped directly under the falling water first, letting the torrent wash over his shoulders, down his chest, and over his member. After a few moments in the falls, Marcus hopped out of the water and shook himself off. “Watch this,” he said as he cannonballed himself back into the pool, sending water everywhere.

I followed his lead more cautiously as I stepped up onto the rocks and under the falls, letting the spray hit my face and soak my hair instantly. The fresh water was colder than I’d expected, sending shivers down my spine, but it felt electrifying. It felt magical. I suddenly felt more relaxed, having not showered since the day we arrived on the island. I dove into the water in front of me and joined Marcus in the pool.

Suddenly, Marcus reached out and splashed me with a handful of water. I yelped, more from surprise than the discomfort, and instinctively retaliated. I splashed him relentlessly, sending water arching through the air toward him. He laughed, deep and unrestrained, and splashed back harder. Our playful exchange continued, water flying everywhere, the mist mixing with our laughter. My chest heaved with both exertion and excitement, adrenaline mixing with the cold of the waterfall.

In the middle of the splashing, my leaf slipped from my fingers and floated away. I froze for a second, my face burning red with embarrassment, but the excitement broke through and I just laughed nervously. The water was already everywhere, the noise of the falls masking everything, and for some reason, I stopped caring.

The leaf drifted, and I let it go, feeling lighter, almost free, the nervous tension I had carried all morning melting into the roaring water around us.

Marcus grinned at me, clearly noticing my initial hesitation. “Relax, Teachy,” he called, his voice echoing off the rocks behind him. “No one’s keeping score here.” I tried to smile, though my heart was still racing, my chest tight from both laughter and the rush of the cold water hitting my skin.

I froze for a moment, my heart skipping a beat, when I noticed something that made my stomach lurch once again. Below the water, Marcus was also fully erect. Heat rushed up my neck and settled in my cheeks. I could feel my pulse thudding in my temples again. My mind wanted to look away, to look at anything else. But my gaze kept sneaking back, betraying me.

Marcus didn’t flinch. He just gave me that confident, almost teasing grin, the same one I’d seen countless times before. He had nothing to be ashamed of, his chest was wide and strong, and his arms flexed naturally as he reached to splash me again, and his erect phallus was beyond impressive. Even in that awkward, electric moment, he looked completely at ease, effortlessly magnetic, and unapologetically himself.

I tried to focus on the feel of the water instead. The cold rush of it over my chest, the way it splashed and ran down my arms, soaking away some of my embarrassment. I was just another body in the water, exposed, vulnerable, and yet somehow not ashamed.

Marcus flicked water at me again, laughing, and I couldn't help but retaliate. We started a small war of splashes, each trying to drench the other, ducking under the waterfall for cover. We stood there in the water, laughing and playing until our stomachs hurt and our voices echoed off the cliff's walls. Water caught the sunlight like a giant glass prism, sprinkling us with rainbow-colored specks that danced across our skin. My laughter came easier than it had in days, raw and unfiltered, a sound that belonged only to the two of us in that secluded clearing.

Every now and then, my eyes would wander to Marcus. His movements were so natural, so fluid, it almost felt like watching someone who was in sync with the water itself. But this time, I didn't care that I was staring at him.

I even found myself laughing more freely, splashing him without hesitation, enjoying the absurdity of it all. The nervous energy that had gripped me the last couple of days melted away under the rush of the waterfall, under the ridiculousness of being here, naked, and unselfconscious with someone I barely understood but somehow became obsessed with.

Every splash, every shout of laughter, every shiver from the cold water drew me further into the moment. I stopped worrying about the leaf that had floated away and exposed my member, stopped worrying about the blush that refused to fade, stopped worrying about whether or not Marcus could see me. Marcus's presence made that entire clearing feel alive. None of this belonged to the outside world; this was our moment, our little chaotic, sunlit bubble of freedom.

We sank deeper into the pool, letting the water rush over us, splashing each other with reckless abandon. Every movement, every laugh, and every glance was amplified in the warm, humid air. The warmth of the sun on our backs contrasted sharply with the cool water rushing over our shoulders, giving me goosebumps. I could feel Marcus beside me, close enough that our shoulders brushed sometimes. I realized I didn't care how my body looked or how it was doing. I was here, present, laughing, and wet, and everything else was just noise.

Eventually, the splashing slowed, but the energy between us still lingered, humming through my chest. We paused, floating in the pool, dripping and catching our breaths, smiling at each other like idiots. Marcus tilted his head back under the waterfall, letting the water pound down his shoulders and chest, and I couldn't help but notice the relaxed way he carried himself. The tension, the self-consciousness, the constant planning for survival, it all seemed to vanish the second we entered this water. Part of me wished we never had to leave, that we could be here for just a little while longer. Alone together.

Chapter Thirteen

We resumed hiking, and struggled through the very hot day. The sun was beating down, and despite the thick leaves and branches hiding the direct sunlight, the jungle floor remained dry and the air stiff. The shower was refreshing, but I began to sweat again. I usually got embarrassed when I sweat in front of people, and I was certainly self-conscious about Marcus seeing my armpit stains.

As we continued walking, I ate a few berries that were leftover from breakfast. Surprisingly, they weren't mushy yet. I scarfed down the handful of berries as I began hearing sounds of branches snapping up ahead.

Marcus and I paused and listened for a moment. The noises stopped. So, we continued on our way, but then, we heard it again. This time, we saw an animal in the distance walking toward us. I stopped because I wasn't sure what it was.

"Marcus, what is that?" I asked.

"I don't know," he replied.

We resumed walking in that direction, assuming it was something small and harmless. We made it about twenty feet before it popped out from behind a tree, directly in our path, staring us down. We stopped and gazed. It was a monkey.

"Aw, it's so cute," I said to Marcus.

"It's fucking ugly," Marcus responded.

"That's rude," I said under my breath.

"What did you say?" Marcus looked over at me.

"Nothing."

We remained still, but the monkey started approaching us. It was making sounds that I always associated with a monkey when I'd hear it on TV, but I never heard them in person. I couldn't tell if it was angry or just wanting to see who we were.

It stopped about five feet from us, and both Marcus and I were unsure what to do.

Do we stay still? Or do we try to show it that we are not harmful?

Marcus remained silent, so I took the lead and slowly stepped toward the monkey. It didn't move; it just stared at me making quiet noises.

"Hey, little dude," I said. Its eyes widened, looking into mine.

"We are trying to go home," I added. "Are you friendly?"

The monkey responded with some louder noises but appeared as if it had a small smile on its face.

"Want to walk with us?" I asked the monkey.

The monkey started to become flustered. I watched as the monkey turned away from us, took a few steps, and then turned back around, as if it were waiting for us to walk with it.

"I think the monkey is scared," I said to Marcus.

"It's just a monkey," Marcus said with a laugh.

"I shouldn't do this, but why not," so I reached out, picked up the monkey, and held it like a baby.

"What are you doing?" Marcus asked.

"Trying to calm it down," I answered.

"What if it has rabies?"

"Too late now. Let's keep walking."

I started walking with the monkey in my arms. It seemed calm now, turning its head to look around the jungle as Marcus walked behind me.

"Are we still heading the right direction?" I asked Marcus.

"Yup, we are," he responded.

"Well, Mr. Monkey, we are taking you on an adventure," I said to the monkey with a laugh.

"How do you know it's a guy?" Marcus asked.

"He doesn't seem to feel threatened, so I'd assume he's a male. If it were a female, it would probably get scared and try to attack us."

"You have way too much time on your hands."

"I just have always been fascinated by animals. They're so different from us, yet so many of their mannerisms are exactly the same."

"Exactly the same? Like we're animals?" he asked.

I laughed, "You for certain, anyways."

The two of us continued on our hike, laughing together.

Chapter Fourteen

After about an hour of hiking and bonding, Marcus and I stumbled upon a large clearing with a crystal-blue river. The vegetation around it was vibrant with life, beautiful colors with flowers bursting full of energy. The only way to the other side seemed to be a wall of logs stopping the water from flowing further.

"What is that?" I asked, pointing to the wall in front of us.

"Looks like a dam," Marcus said.

"A damn what?" I asked, chuckling.

"Very funny, smart guy," Marcus smirked. "But I think we're going to have to cross that to get back."

"Why don't we go through the dry part down there?" I asked him, pointing down at the seemingly dry land where the other side of the river had dried up.

"Look," Marcus began, pointing just past the dam. "If we went down there, there'd be no way to get back up and climb to the other side. No roots, no makeshift ladder, nothing."

"Oh…" I said, "You're right."

We walked to the water's edge and looked around. I looked down into the water. It looked deep and murky. I probably wouldn't be able to make it back up if I fell into it.

"This thing is going to be tough to cross," I said to Marcus. "But I think we can make it."

"You're strong. You can handle it," he said with a laugh.

I looked at my monkey, still chewing on a leaf as it lay curled up in my arms. I rested him over my shoulder and let him wrap his arms around me.

"You ready?" I asked Marcus.

"As ready as I'll ever be," he said, taking the first step onto the log. "How about you?"

"I think so," I replied.

The dam wasn't what I expected. From a distance, it looked almost peaceful. I thought it was flat logs stretching across the narrowest part of the river, but the moment we stepped onto it, I realized how slick the surface really was. Every step demanded complete focus. The roar of rushing water next to us echoed in my ears. Cold mist sprayed up from below, and every few seconds I had to blink it from my eyes just to see where I was going.

Marcus led the way, his boots finding small patches of dry stone between the darker, gleaming sections of log. He moved slowly, balancing his weight as best he could, glancing back at me every few steps. “Careful,” he called over the roar. “It’s a little slippery!”

“Yeah, I noticed!” I shouted back, trying to sound braver than I felt inside. My heart thudded against my chest, and I kept my arms out at my sides to try and keep better balance. The river below was violent, white foam spilling over rocks like claws waiting to drag me under.

We were halfway across when I made the mistake of looking into the jungle, just for a second. The trees were tall and green, glistening in the sunlight that managed to cut through the mist. It was almost beautiful enough to forget where I was. Before I realized it, I did. My boot slipped.

“Woah!” The world fell in an instant. I felt my leg skid forward, water surging over the edge, and before I could process what was happening, the rest of me followed. My stomach dropped as my foot slid off the edge of the log, about to hit the water below.

“Noah!” Marcus yelled as his hand clamped around my wrist, pulling me back. My other hand scrambled for safety, slapping against the water.

The roar of the river grew deafening, the sound swallowing my fear whole. Marcus's grip held firm, muscles straining as he leaned back, pulling me toward him. "Don't move!" he barked, "Be still." His fingernails dug into my wrist with his harsh grip, bringing me back to the world again. I gasped, water dripping from my face, the cold air biting my skin. My feet scrambled for footing on the narrow slick ledge, and with one last pull, Marcus dragged me upright and into his chest.

For a heartbeat, we just stood there, my chest pressed against his, his arm tight around me. Our faces were just inches apart, close enough for me to see the tiny droplets of water clinging to his eyelashes, to feel his breath against my face. My pulse was racing; I couldn't tell if it was fear or something else. "Th-thank you, Marcus."

We both exhaled at the same time. Then Marcus let out a shaky laugh. "You really know how to keep things interesting, huh?"

"I just wanted to test your reflexes," I said, teasing him.

"Yeah, well," he said, still catching his breath, "you almost tested how good I am at fishing bodies out of freezing cold rivers."

"Well if it's anything like fishing bodies out of the ocean after they're consumed by the waves, I'm not gonna hold my breath!" I replied cheekily.

We both laughed, half out of nerves and half out of relief. He loosened his hold on me, though his hand lingered a moment longer than it needed to before pulling away. "Let's keep moving," he said finally, voice softer now. "One step at a time."

I nodded, forcing my legs to steady. Together we continued across the dam, moving slower this time. We took our steps as steadily as we could. The rush of the river stayed loud beneath us, but now, instead of fear, I felt a quiet certainty in the space between us. It became something quiet and certain in the space between us.

The last stretch across the dam was chaos held together by sheer will. The rush of the wind and water was so fierce it quickly got hard to breathe. To keep our balance, (and for no other reason at all) Marcus held my hand as we crossed the last bit of the dam. I'd lost count over how many times I'd almost lost my footing, thankful I had Marcus there to keep me safe. The monkey held tightly to my neck, thankful not only for me, but for Marcus by extension. By the time we reached the river bank, I was ready to fall to my knees.

The second my boots touched solid ground, I dropped to my knees, breathing hard and loud. My palms were scraped from gripping the logs, and my clothes clung tight to my body, soaked through from the mist. Behind me, Marcus climbed down the last ledge, steady and sure as ever. His hair plastered to his forehead, his shoulders rose and fell with every breath.

"You made it," Marcus said with a smile. "I knew you could do it!"

"That was so scary," I replied.

The monkey jumped down from my shoulder and onto the ground, chirping as if to agree. He was shaking, clearly terrified from the whole endeavor.

"I'm happy you're okay," Marcus said. "We—sorry, I'm happy we're okay."

I smiled at Marcus, "I'm happy we're okay, too."

"Wow!" Marcus gave me a cheeky smile as he looked at the dam behind us. "That was borderline suicidal!"

"Say what you want," I chuckled at him. "But I think I've found my new favorite hobby!"

Marcus laughed, like I was the funniest guy in the world. "Uh, you better do some practicing if 'Extreme Dam Crossing' is going to be your new thing. Because you almost became Taveuni's dam victim number one!"

"Hey, if it means getting off this island!" I joked, laughing.

He smirked at that, but his eyes softened. "Don't joke like that, you scared the hell out of me."

For a moment, neither of us spoke. The only sound was the roar of the river behind us and the wind weaving through the trees. Then, wordlessly, Marcus reached forward and brushed me off. His fingers brushed my collarbone, quick and clumsy, and he looked away almost immediately after our eyes met.

The jungle on the other side was much more muddy but calmer, sheltered by tall trees that swayed gently in the wind. The air smelled of rain and earth, it was almost nice. My legs still trembled from the crossing, but the deeper into the jungle we went, the quieter everything became.

"It's so pretty out here," Marcus began. "So many beautiful sights." I almost blushed as he said that, looking at me ever so slightly.

"It's not terrible…" I replied. "But next time, maybe we don't take the scenic route. Too much danger for my taste."

"We'll see…" he said.

The undergrowth cleared a bit ahead, leading toward another dense stretch of jungle. The roar of the dam faded behind us, replaced by the rhythmic sound of water dripping from the leaves above. I let out a long breath I hadn't realized I was holding. It was time to relax for a bit and enjoy the peaceful walk through the trees.

Chapter Fifteen

The jungle felt hotter by the hour, like the trees were leaning in closer with each step we took. Sweat glued my shirt to my back, and even though Marcus tried to keep our pace steady, I could tell he was just as tired as I was. The difference between us was how hot he looked when he was drenched in sweat.

My small monkey friend had clung to my shoulder for most of the trek, restless and twitchy. Its little fingers tugging at my collar every time a vine brushed too close to us. By the time the shadows stretched long and the last streaks of sunlight filtered through the canopy, its squealing started again. Nothing but shrill bursts that made us both wince.

I tried to soothe him by running a hand along his back, but the monkey just twisted in agitation, as if it sensed something ahead that I couldn't see. That's when the outline of a wooden hut came into view, tucked in a clearing where the undergrowth thinned out. The hut looked like it had been swallowed by the jungle years ago. Its roof was sagging, the walls eaten through in places, one side almost buried beneath tangled roots and vines. Marcus and I approached with caution.

"Would you look at that..." Marcus let out a low breath. "Looks abandoned," he muttered, squinting through the afterglow. He pushed a palm against the wall as the boards groaned. The monkey squealed louder, scurrying up to the top of my shoulders, his tiny body trembling like it wanted nothing to do with the place.

"Monkey doesn't seem to like it..." I glanced at Marcus. "You think someone's still using it?"

He shook his head, though not with much certainty. "Nobody's been here in years. This hut belongs to the earth now. But we need to take a rest break, and as decrepit as it is, it's a shelter."

My body ached at the thought, but unease prickled under my skin. My monkey's squeals echoed through the trees, sharp enough they scattered a few nearby birds off their perches. It was almost like he was warning us, unsure if the hut would bring relief—or danger. "I don't know..." I finally replied.

Marcus wiped his forehead with the back of his hand for what had to be the hundredth time, but it didn't do much good. Sweat poured down his temples, soaking into the collar of his shirt until it clung to his chest. He looked absolutely wrecked by the heat, every muscle in his arms and neck shining under the fading light. I shouldn't have found that so sexy, but I did. Even worn out, even with dirt smudged along his jaw, there was something magnetic about the way Marcus carried himself through all of this.

"Teachy, please," he said, voice rough and low. "Tell me we can take this rest break! I will carry you the rest of the way if it means we can spend the night here!"

I couldn't help the smile tugging at my mouth, though I tried to hide it. The monkey shifted on my shoulder, chittering and chirping softly in response to Marcus's plea. I let out a slow breath, rolling my sore shoulders. "I suppose we've got enough time left to make it back to the village in time. And Monkey seems won over for the time being. But we'll need to move first thing at sunrise!"

"Thank you," Marcus said as he walked into the crooked doorway of the hut, "And please, for the love of God, leave your monkey friend outside." His tone wasn't sharp exactly, but there was enough edge in it to make my stomach flip.

"What?" I turned, shielding the little creature almost instinctively. Its beady eyes blinked up at me, and for a second I thought I saw some kind of trust there. "We're in the middle of the jungle! I don't want him to get eaten by something!" I protested, hugging the monkey close.

Marcus gave me a judgmental look. The kind of look I could tell he gave just because he thought I was being stubborn to spite him. "Anything that comes close to him is gonna be scared off by his constant screaming. Not to mention the fact that he found us. This is his natural habitat. He will be fine." He waved a hand at the monkey, who was still shaking as it clung to me.

It's not like the constant screaming didn't bother me. The truth was, I was annoyed, too. The sharp little cries drilled into my mind, bouncing off the walls of the abandoned hut and making it impossible to focus on anything else. The thought of trying to rest with that racket inside was unbearable. I sighed, finally loosening my hold on the squirming little guy. "Fair enough. He stays outside tonight."

After a while of settling in, the night swallowed the jungle. The only light inside the hut came from the moon shining through a jagged hole in the ceiling above us. A chunk of the roof was just gone, leaving a window to the stars endless against the black sky. If it weren't for the stars, I couldn't tell where the darkness of the hut ended and the night outside began.

Marcus and I had unfortunately (fortunately) been reduced to sharing the sole moldy cot and pillow that the shelter had for us. It was bigger than a twin but smaller than a queen, the kind of bed that felt just a little too tight for two grown men but not enough to justify one of us sleeping on the dirty, dusty floor. The old fabric creaked every time we shifted, his arm brushing mine when he reached behind his head. I could smell the salt of his skin, the faint musk of sweat and leaves clinging to him after the day's hike.

We both stared upward, our chests rising and falling in rhythm, though I was painfully aware of every inch of space (the little there was) between us. The stars looked brighter here than they ever had back home, unblocked by the light pollution of the city, unfiltered by anything but the wide jungle canopy broken open above us. It was almost scary to think just how little I was in the grand scheme of it all.

"I feel so small," I said quietly. The words tumbled out before I had time to tuck them away. "So small and alone in the world right now. On this island, it's like…" I trailed off, searching for the right way to shape the thought. "Like the sky is pressing down on me, reminding me I don't belong here. I'm trying, Marcus, but I'm having such a hard time just belonging right now."

The truth stuck in my throat, bitter as I forced it out. Every day here was a battle—either against the hunger that gnawed at my stomach, against the way my legs shook after miles of trudging through endless jungle, or against the constant fear that we'd make one wrong step and never find our way back. It got to the point where I sometimes found myself longing for things I never thought I'd miss. The sounds of traffic, fluorescent lights, even the cold hum of a big refrigerator.

I rolled onto my side toward Marcus, my cheek brushing against the rough pillow. The sight of Marcus's profile against the starlight made my throat tighten. His jaw looked steady, his breath even, he made me feel safe. Almost like I was home already. "I can't wait to be home," I whispered, almost to myself.

Marcus shifted beside me, his head turning just enough for me to catch the curve of his smile in the moonlight. His eyes lingered on me in that steady way of his, the kind that made it hard to look away. "Hey, hey, you're okay. You've just gotta remind yourself you're in control," he said, his voice low, like he was sharing something he'd learned the hard way. "You just have to ground yourself."

I blinked at him, my chest still tight from everything I'd spilled out in the moment. Ground myself. The words felt foreign here, where so much of my life now was dictated by the island, how could I ground myself here? This hellish island controlled when the sun rose, when it burned hardest down on us, when the bugs decided to swarm, or even when my stomach twisted with hunger pains. Control was something I didn't think I had anymore. Not here.

"How can I ground myself here?" I asked him. "I hate this island."

Marcus didn't press further. Instead, he slid his arm and let it hang lazily off the side of the cot. His fingers brushed against the soft dirt floor and dug them into it, slow and deep. "When I need to ground myself, I feel the earth around me." He raked his fingertips through the grit and sand, making a soft, scratching sound in the silence. His shoulders relaxed, and he let out a breath. "It doesn't matter where you are, as long as you remember that you're in control."

A small smirk tugged at my mouth despite myself. I reached over the edge, too, my fingers curling into the cool sand. The grains slipped easily between them, some sticking to the sweat on my skin. It was rough, but it was grounding, real in a way that felt almost new in the turmoil I'd been living through.

"See? Doesn't that feel nice?" Marcus asked, his eyes on me again, his smile turning softer, almost teasing.

"I guess," I said, trying to sound relaxed.

The two of us stayed like that for what felt like forever. Just stretched out on the cot, arms dangling over the edge, fingers buried in the sand. We let the grains shift between our fingertips as we lay there. The sound of sand sliding over itself became strangely comforting, like a soothing rhythm that anchored me down instead of letting my thoughts drift too far away.

The roof above us had long since fallen away in some places, but that missing chunk didn't feel like ruin, it felt more like a window. A jagged frame opening up to a piece of the universe above us. The sky stretched on forever, an endless sprawl of stars so sharp and vivid it almost hurt to look at them for too long. I followed Marcus's gaze upward, and for a moment, I felt like the world had quieted just for us. It worked—I had calmed down because of Marcus. For the first time in a long time, I felt at peace.

Then Marcus spoke, his voice low, "Isn't it wild to think there are more grains of sand on this beach than there are stars up in the sky?"

"That's not even close to right!" I couldn't help but burst out laughing at his statement. The sound filled the hut and startled even me, but I couldn't help it. The thought of Marcus trying to be all profound and getting it mixed up was too much. My stomach clenched as I kept laughing, my hand pressing over my mouth like that would muffle it. "I think you've got that the other way around," I managed, still grinning so hard my cheeks ached.

"How can you be so sure? You ever counted?" Marcus tilted his head toward me, eyebrows raised. He didn't try to defend himself, just let my laughter wash over him. "We'll have to fact-check that when we get back," he said with a small chuckle, his hand dragging through the sand once again. "But no matter what, I think we can agree there's a ton of both! Like the sky is full of all those grains of sand. Kinda amazing."

"Yeah," I murmured, letting the laughter fade into something quieter, something softer as my eyes drifted back up to the stars. In that moment, with Marcus lying close enough for me to feel the heat radiating from his shoulder, everything seemed sharper, fuller, too real to deny. "It is," I finally said "All the grains of sand in the sky…"

Chapter Sixteen

Beep. Beep. Beep. The sound of my alarm jolted me awake. The blinds blocked most of the sunlight, but enough slipped through to fill the room. It took me a moment to realize I was in my own room—my room back in California.

"W-what? I'm home?" I sat up in my bed; it was always too comfortable for me. Much more comfortable than anything I knew in Fiji. If it had ever actually been Fiji. I looked around. "Marcus?"

Was it all a dream? Had I just slept for several days? What was going on?

"Honey, come down for breakfast!" Suddenly, I heard a knock on my door. I turned as the doorknob slowly twisted, the squeaky door inching open toward me. It stopped after a few inches. "My goodness, you've been sleeping so soundly!"

I felt a twitch in my heart as I realized it was my mother's voice. I rubbed my eyes without looking up at her. “Yeah, I guess I did…” I scratched my head, thinking perhaps I’d lost my mind and forgotten the concept of time itself. “I’m not sure what happened. What’s for breakfast, Mom?”

“We’re having pancakes and bacon,” she declared as the door pushed further open, and a shadow began to emerge from the light. The silhouette was familiar—my mother’s. I recognized her by the sweater she wore. But when she stepped fully into the room, it wasn’t her. The body was my mother’s, but the face was not. Her face, still half-hidden in shadow, was squarer—more masculine.

“What the fuck!” I yelled.

“Good morning, Noah,” she said.

Then it clicked—it was Marcus’s face on my mother’s body. I curled up on my bed in fear. “What is going on?!”

My own screams jolted me back into reality. I sat up, sweating, and on high alert. I realized that I was not back home in California. I was still in Fiji, with Marcus beside me. Relief flooded through me—I was glad to be here, glad that my mother didn’t have Marcus’s face.

Chapter Seventeen

In the middle of the night, I awoke with a start. The moon was just past its peak, meaning it was likely an hour or so after midnight. I deliberated whether or not I should return to sleep but ultimately decided against it, as we'd undoubtedly be walking again in only a couple of hours. Yawning, I looked over at Marcus, who was facing away from me, still fast asleep.

I had decided to sleep in my shirt, dirty as it was, and Marcus had decided to sleep only in his Calvin Klein underwear, bulging at the seams. I couldn't help but stare at the way his underwear cupped his muscular body, reinforcing all of the muscle underneath.

Suddenly, as I lay there lost in my fantasies of Marcus and me, the cot shifted. Marcus turned over, facing me for a moment before he placed his head on my shoulder and wrapped his arm around my chest.

I felt my face become tingly; blood rushed into every part of my body. I wanted Marcus to fuck me. I was so horny—I wanted him bad. I knew he wanted me, too. I felt the thickness that filled up my pants, and I knew it wasn't going to go away on its own.

"Marcus?" I asked. "Are you awake?" Secretly I'd hoped not. If he was awake, he might realize what he was doing and stop. I didn't want this to ever stop.

In response, Marcus reached up and put his fingers over my lips, shushing me. "I'm exhausted, Teachy… Let me rest." He said, half asleep.

Then, he climbed onto me, positioned his head onto my chest, and lifted one of my legs up and wrapped it around his waist. I scooted down, our hips meeting at the same place. I wrapped my arms around his ribcage, feeling the muscle that I had only ever visually dreamed about. Now, I was feeling it, and he was feeling me. "Marcus…"

Suddenly, as I turned down to face Marcus, our lips met before I could get another word out. He pressed his mouth hard against mine and I didn't hold back. I slid my tongue through his lips and fought for dominance. A battle I was more than happy to lose as I let Marcus's tongue explore every inch of my mouth. His breath was hot against mine, but I didn't care. The only thing I cared about at the moment was tangling our tongues further together.

His hands began to run up and down my chest, and our kisses became frequent and intimate. He kissed my lips, my cheeks, my neck, all so passionately. After a few more, Marcus put his entire body weight on me, and we laid there for a moment, taking it all in.

I felt something poking between my legs, and I felt it move when Marcus moved. I felt it throbbing during every passing second. Marcus started kissing my neck, and I couldn't help but moan.

"You like that?" Marcus asked, whispering into my ear.

"Yes, I do. I really like it," I replied in pleasure.

I could feel my self-control leaking from me as we lay there. His hand slipped underneath my shirt, and he slid my shirt up toward my neck, exposing my body underneath.

"You're so beautiful," he said to me. "I could get used to this."

I felt Marcus pull my shirt up, so I decided to save him the work and take it off myself. I watched in amazement as he did the same with his. We quickly resumed the soft kisses all over our lips and necks. Kissing his neck made him throb more intensely, and I knew he wanted to fuck me.

My hands slid down Marcus's waist, and they stopped at the waistband of his underwear. I started rubbing my finger and playing with his waistband, and it turned Marcus on more and more each time.

"You're so sexy. I can't resist you," I said to Marcus.

"Oh, yeah," he responded. "Can I take your shorts off? I'm not wearing mine. It's only fair…" he said.

"Take them off me," I began. "Please."

In one swift motion, Marcus lifted my legs into the air and slid my shorts off. "I've been waiting to do this since the waterfall!"

I pulled him close and kissed him again. "I've been wanting you to do this since the waterfall," I smirked.

"Then let us not waste any more time," he responded, resuming everything that made me twitch and want him more.

I felt him slide my Jockey underwear down my legs before he threw them on the ground. He then started to slide his Calvin Kleins down, and I couldn't help but see his bulge emerge from underneath his underwear. He slid them down to his knees, picked up his legs, and fully unclothed. I watched as he continued to grow, and I knew he wanted this as much as I did.

Feeling the same way, I felt myself begin to stiffen when he pressed his naked body against mine. I felt his bulge slide against mine, and his kisses along my neck made me want him inside me already.

I felt him kiss down my chest and onto my groin. He grabbed a hold of my stiff erection and placed his lips around it softly. He began going down on me in a way that I never experienced before. He knew what he was doing, and he was good at it. I moaned and felt myself twitch inside his mouth. I ran my hands through his hair as he picked up his pace.

After a few minutes of jaw-dropping pleasure, he kissed his way back up to my lips, and asked, "Would you like to taste me?"

"I really want to," I replied.

He rolled over, adjusted how he was laying, helped me climb onto him, and ran his hands all over my body as I began by sucking on his neck. I kissed my way down to his upper chest, admiring his muscular pecs. I continued down, feeling how beautiful he was, before I arrived at his fully exposed erection. His brown pubic hairs were beautiful and freshly trimmed. I grabbed a hold of his dick, licked up and down, before wrapping my mouth around it and reciprocating what he did to me.

He moaned in a way that made me speed up and give him what he deserved. He ran his hands through my hair, just like I did to him. After a few minutes, he pulled me off and brought my lips back up to his to kiss him some more.

"I want to have you," Marcus said. "All of you."

"You can have me," I replied.

Marcus took a hold of me, put me on my back, got on top of me, and watched him lift my legs up. I thought he was just going to use me, but he seemed to have more in mind first. I watched as his face buried in between my legs. I moaned so hard, and I could tell it was turning Marcus on more and more each time.

"I'm gonna fuck you so good," Marcus said after spitting on my hole.

"I'm ready," I whispered.

I watched as he spit on his dick, spread it all over, and aligned it with my hole. I felt a soft pinch as he began pressing it into me. He slid himself inside me, easing into my tightness.

"Go slow," I pleaded.

"I will," he said under his breath. "Don't worry."

I let out a soft moan, and I eased into his thickness. I held onto him as he took the lead in pleasuring the both of us. He pushed himself further inside me now than he did just moments ago. I gripped onto his hips, letting him enjoy all of me. My moans became frequent, and his thrusts went deeper.

"Do you like that?" Marcus asked.

"You feel so good," I whispered to him.

We continued for a few minutes in the same position before he lifted me off of him, laid me on my stomach, got behind me, and slid himself back inside.

"I'm gonna cum soon," he said with a moan. "I want to cum inside you."

"Do it," I begged.

I felt him speed up, hold me tighter, go deeper, and within a few moments, I felt his warm ejaculation fill me up. Marcus thrusted a few more times before stopping and softly pulled himself out of me.

"Do you want to fuck me?" he asked.

"Do you want me to?" I asked.

"Yes," he began softly, "I do."

Marcus got in the same position I was; his body laid on his stomach, ass up, ready for me. I spread his legs a bit and admired how well groomed he was. It's like he was wanting this to happen to him. I spit on it, the same as he did for me, before I pressed myself inside him.

"I'm really tight. Please start slow," he said.

"Of course," I said.

I felt as I slowly inched further inside of him, hearing his moans every time more of me went inside. He pushed himself back toward me. "That feels so good," he said.

"Oh yeah?" I asked.

At this point, I was fully inside him. I started thrusting, letting him ease into it. He was so tight.

"Harder," he begged.

I sped up the pace and went as deep as I could. Marcus started moaning harder, and I could feel myself about to climax. After a few minutes of feeling immense pleasure from him, I pressed my chest against his back and moaned into his ear while saying, "I'm gonna cum soon."

"Cum inside me, Noah," he said.

I kept going, and I thrusted a few times as I felt myself burst inside him. I moaned, too, feeling something I hadn't felt in a long time. I slowly pulled out of him, and we laid next to each other, staring each other in the eyes.

"That felt really good," Marcus said.

"It was. You felt amazing," I added. "All of you did."

We were both out of breath, so we remained still for a few moments before Marcus asked, "Will you spoon me?"

"Yeah," I said.

Marcus turned over, bent his legs, and I cuddled up behind him, holding him in my arms. I kissed his neck as we lay there in pure bliss. Everything about this moment was perfect. Everything about him was perfect.

Chapter Eighteen

The sun was shining, and I woke up in Marcus's arms. My slight shuffling made Marcus wake up, too. We looked each other in the eyes and smiled. He was cuddling me, and I could feel his body against mine. He moved a little bit, and I felt him poke into my thigh. I brushed it off and continued feeling his warmth around me.

I turned toward Marcus, and we locked eyes for what felt like forever. I couldn't peel my eyes away from his. My nose was close enough that I could smell his curly hair. I kissed his cheek, and he smiled at me. I never felt closer to him until now.

Afterwards, we got up and got dressed. Watching him slip his shirt over his chest while wearing his black Calvin Kleins made me have to get dressed quickly to hide the evidence in my pants. After we got dressed, I could see the outline of Marcus's bulge through his pants. I no longer felt the need to cover up, so I rested my pants by my side and continued on.

We walked out of the hut, and Marcus was sure to hold the door open for me. Little gestures like that made me feel like I belonged with him. The monkey was sleeping on the roof of the hut. I began to feel attached to it, so I hoped he would still be there when I woke up in the morning. The monkey woke up to the sound of the door to the hut slamming closed. I reached up for the monkey, placed him into my arms, and rubbed his head while his arms clung to me.

I wanted to name the monkey, but Marcus insisted that I not. He was against the idea; he didn't want me to pay any more attention to the thing. He said it would be too tough for me to say goodbye once we got back to the village.

"I really want to name the monkey," I said to Marcus. "I can't keep just calling him 'Monkey'… What about Abu?"

"If you really *have* to name it, don't name it that," Marcus replied. "That's dumb."

"Okay," I began. "What about Bananas?"

Marcus laughed. "Too cliche. Also monkeys don't even like bananas that much."

"Hm…" I thought, "Debbie? That could be funny!"

Marcus grimaced, "Who the fuck names their pet monkey Debbie?"

"Okay, what about George? I've always wanted a pet named George."

"Actually, I don't hate that. Kinda reminds me of *Curious George.*"

"That's what I was going for! His name shall be George," I said while looking down and smiling at my newest friend.

Marcus and I began our daily excursion, holding hands the entire time. Every so often, we would lock eyes and smile as we ventured through the jungle. Behind Marcus's sparkly blue eyes were vibrant trees and flowers, which I hadn't really appreciated much until now. It was beautiful.

The forest green vines blended well with the bright white flower petals. Occasionally, we would walk past a colorful bush that was overloaded with berries, which we would be sure to take a few to snack on during our journey back to the village. Many of the fruit bushes had multi-colored butterflies flying around, and I wondered if they thought I was a giant monster coming to disturb them.

Marcus and I continued hiking through the vibrant green forest, his hand holding mine. He took me by surprise when he was the one who grabbed my hand. After I finished smiling and being caught up in the moment, I thought to myself: We *should* be back to the village by morning. Part of me did not want to get back to the village so I could spend time with Marcus, but I also had a plane to catch.

"This journey is about to be over," I said to Marcus. "We're almost back."

"Yeah, we are," he said. "Part of me is gonna miss all this."

"Yeah?" I asked.

"Yeah… Being out here, surviving with you. It's taught me a lot about being there for someone," he began, "It's taught me a lot about myself…"

"Like what?"

Marcus seemed to struggle for a moment before responding. It was as if he had to force himself to speak the words he wanted to say. "Noah, there's something I have to tell you."

"What is it?"

"I really like you. I'm sorry that I didn't tell you that sooner. I've liked you since the moment I met you in the airport," he began. "Being with you, I felt like I belong here on this island, and that's all because of you. I wish we had more time out here together."

I didn't know what to say. I've never fallen for someone as fast as I fell for Marcus, and now hearing he felt the same was like a dream come true. "I like you, too, Marcus. And I wish we had more time out here together too. But we have to keep moving, I can't miss that plane home. I miss my life way too much… I'm so sorry, Marcus." I said, tearing up.

"I know…" Marcus looked sad for a moment. I could see the tears forming in the corners of his eyes. After a few moments of quiet thinking, he seemed to have an "aha" moment. "Wait a minute…"

"What is it?" I said, looking at him curiously.

"Noah, there's something else I have to tell you. Something important. Something you have to promise you won't be mad at me for telling you." Marcus seemed serious. More serious than I'd seen him before. But as he spoke this time, he stopped us in our tracks and looked me in the eyes, his hands on my chest. "Do you promise?"

"Marcus, whatever it is I'm sure I'll understand…" I put my hands around his forearms. "It's gonna be okay. Whatever it is, we'll talk through it together."

Marcus took a deep breath in before he spoke. I could hear his heart pounding in his chest. "Noah, I'm not really a missionary."

"You…what?" I asked, a pit suddenly forming in my stomach. "What do you mean?"

"I took the missionary job because I needed a fresh start. I needed to get away from California and there was no other way." Marcus smirked, chuckling to himself. "I lied to the church so I could start a new life somewhere."

"But- why didn't you just go back to Rhode Island?" I asked, the pit growing larger.

"There's nothing for me in Rhode Island anymore. My family disowned me when they found out I was gay. My mom and dad kicked me out, even my brother wanted nothing to do with me anymore. The truth is, I came out to California to be with the man I thought was the love of my life. But after he broke my heart, I had nothing and nobody."

"But, you, uh…" I couldn't find the words.

"I came out here to find a new life. To find a new me!" Marcus exclaimed.

My heart was breaking. "You lied to me…?"

Marcus laughed, almost scaringly. "It doesn't matter, Noah, none of that matters now!"

"What do you mean?" I asked, shaking.

"I'm not under a contract. I can go back to California and be with you!"

"What do you mean? Victor said you were supposed to stay here for the whole year. He said the church sent you here as a missionary. What will Victor say? What will the church say? Is impersonating a missionary a crime?"

"It doesn't matter, I'm not a missionary, I'm not tied down here. And who cares what they think? We'll have a fresh start together in California together."

"Why did you lie to everyone?" I asked him. "Why did you lie to me?" I couldn't believe what I was hearing. I started walking away from Marcus. I couldn't be with Marcus a second longer. These past few days, I thought he was the person I could trust above anyone else in this world. But it turned out he was lying to me the whole time we were together. "I can't believe this…"

I decided I would finish the journey back to the village alone. I didn't need a liar guiding me anymore. I could make it the rest of the way on my own, and surely he could too. At the very least, he could lie to himself that he could make it back. I was now several yards away from Marcus, but I could hear his footsteps walking toward me. I began to run from him. From his lies.

"Noah, don't go," I heard Marcus say from a distance. "Please."

"Just leave me alone..." I called back, but I didn't look. I kept running. Alone.

Chapter Nineteen

As I pushed my way through the vegetation, every branch and vine seemed heavier than the last. Even without Marcus, I didn't feel the least bit alone. George clung to my shoulder, his tiny fingers digging tightly into the fabric of my shirt. His usual chattering had been replaced by low, restless squeaks that mirrored the sorrowful mood pressing down on both of us. The air was thick, but not in the lively, humid way it was the last couple of days. It felt stale and gray now. It was like the world itself had dulled to match the feelings inside my chest.

The canopy above me used to feel so alive, bursting with light, colors, and movement alike. Now it was nothing but a patchwork of shadows and clouds, stitched together by gloom that seemed to smother the sky. I tried to keep my eyes down most of the time, on the mud that caked my shoes and on the uneven ground that pulled at my ankles.

Sweat trickled down my spine as I walked, exhausted. It made my shirt cling to me in damp, cold patches, reminding me of how long I'd been moving without rest. I told myself I couldn't stop, that I wouldn't stop, but the truth was I didn't want to give myself the chance to stop and think about the fact that I was all alone with George in the winding jungle.

The hike was near impossible now, not because of the mud sucking at my boots, but because of what Marcus had done. Because Marcus had lied. The words he spoke still echoed in my mind, clear as if he were walking beside me now, and I hated how much power he still held over me. He lied. He looked right at me and lied, and I had been too blinded by love to see it coming. That cut deeper than anything else. I wanted to feel empathetic for his situation. I could only imagine what it was like to have a family who doesn't keep you in their lives once they find out you aren't like most people. I was fortunate to have a loving family who supported me since I came out when I was fourteen. With that, I was still furious with Marcus.

I clenched my fists until my nails dug into my palms, telling myself I didn't need him. I could keep moving without Marcus. I could survive without Marcus. I did not need Marcus. But every time I repeated it, it sounded less true.

But yet, no matter how hard I tried to convince myself it was true, my chest burned with betrayal. Marcus chose to deceive me, he knew what he was doing, and yet he still did it. I told myself this again and again. I knew I didn't deserve the pain, so why couldn't I stop thinking about him?

From my shoulder, George began shifting uneasily. Without warning, he let out another high-pitched squeal, the sound echoing through the trees. I turned to my side, expecting to see Marcus covering his ears or making a face, but there was nothing there. It was just me, George, and the ringing in my ears.

Chapter Twenty

After a couple hours of hiking, just George and I, we were finally making progress. The colors were still as dull as the moment I left Marcus. The birds didn't sing, the wind didn't dance, the flowers didn't bloom. It was just me on my mission now. We were closing in on the base of the mountain, if we walked through the night, we might just make it with time to spare.

George shifted on my shoulders again as the light rain from above fell down on us, his tiny claws pinching the fabric of my shirt. His fur was damp, making him shiver from the cold. Even his usual pattern of screeching and chatter had faded, as if the weight of my problems were taking their toll on him now too.

My legs continued to ache as I climbed over roots and rocks. It was so tiring, but I didn't slow down. I couldn't slow down. Stopping would lead to thinking, and thinking would lead back to him.

As hard as it was without Marcus, I kept telling myself I didn't need him. Maybe eventually I'd believe it.

Every tree I passed looked the same now. Tall, grayish-brown trunks rising up into the canopy of wet leaves. The sky was gray and clouded, almost as much as I felt inside right now. The sprinkles of rain turned the air cold against my skin and my shirt damp. At least I didn't have to worry about sweating through my shirt again. George clung tighter to me every time the thunder roared through the sky.

"Ow!" My little monkey friend began to squirm once again, his claws digging deeper into my skin than they had before. In an instant, he changed his demeanor now from calm and downtrodden to berserk, hollering and screaming louder than ever before. His cries challenged the thunder itself. "George, what the hell? Can you just calm down for one minute and let me walk through this endless jungle in peace!"

I tried to ignore him, but George just wouldn't stop. George moved from my shoulders and closer to my head. He tugged at my ear, his tiny body against me, and I broke. A sob broke out of me before I could choke it down. I let my knees fall to the mud as I cried. Between Marcus betraying me and George driving me insane, I just couldn't take it anymore. I pressed my palms hard into the earth in a half-hearted attempt to anchor myself there.

Tears burned in my eyes, falling faster than the rain. Everything I'd been holding back, the hurt, the anger, the loneliness, all of it poured out into one ugly rush. I wanted George to stop screaming, I wanted the jungle to stop pressing in, I wanted Marcus's lies to not affect me anymore, but most of all, I wanted to not feel so goddamn small right now.

I dragged the back of my arm across my cheek, smearing my tears and rainwater into a single, wet mess. My heart still raced from my sudden outburst as I tried to steady my breathing and calm down. George, taking another break from yelling, chirped at me softly and nonverbally questioned my state of sadness.

"I'm sorry, buddy," I whispered, "I didn't mean to snap at you like that." George blinked at me and clung softly to my side. I could tell he forgave me. I just wished I could forgive myself.

Suddenly, a deep roar escaped my insides. It caught me off guard for a moment before I realized what it meant: I was starving. And after all this time since our last stop, George probably was too.

I sat there on the ground for a moment, letting the raindrops pour over me as I thought, trying to decide where to begin. I let my eyes scan the jungle floor but found nothing except mud, leaves, sticks, and a pile of something near the base of a nearby tree that caught my attention.

Standing up, I walked toward the strange pile before realizing what it was. They were dark, round, and decaying. They were papayas. “Yes!”

I reached down and grabbed a shriveled, dried-up papaya buried slightly into the dirt. The thing looked like it had been rotting for weeks now. “Well, here goes nothing,” I said, wrinkling my nose. I turned the shriveled papaya over in my hands, tapping it lightly on the ground as if preparing it for a bigger plan. Then, without any warning, I swung my arm and flung it upward. My eyes followed the arc it made into the branches, waiting for a *thud* that never came.

“Alright, let’s try this again.” I turned the shriveled fruit over in my hands once more, ready to try again. I swung my arm and flung it upward toward the bounty and waited another second. Nothing.

“One more time...” I turned the fruit in my hands for the final time. I swung my arm hard and flung it toward the canopy, waiting faintly for something, anything to fall. Nothing.

I let out a long, exaggerated sigh, as I scooped George off my shoulder and held him against my chest. “I know, buddy. I know you’re hungry. So am I…” I said, my stomach growling. “But we’ve gotta keep moving. Just a little farther and we'll get to the village. We're almost there, I promise."

George gave a soft, pitiful squeak in reply. His small hands clutched the fabric of my damp shirt. He looked up at me, and for a second, I swore he actually understood.

"Yeah," I whispered, forcing a smile I didn't really feel, "almost there."

Chapter Twenty-One

The sun set over the horizon as the storm continued to pass, and I was still hiking as much as I could before wrapping up for the night. George had been by my side the entire time. There were a few times that I thought he was going to run away, but it seems that we have developed a sense of companionship with each other.

We were both dodging the rain, trying to stay dry under as many trees as possible. He would occasionally let out some cries while shaking off the excess rainwater. If only we'd had an umbrella to shield us from some of the water.

Hunger gnawed at me, and I could tell George felt it too. George was starting to become frantic again. I wasn't sure what to do, because he couldn't tell me what was wrong.

"Um. What's wrong, George. Are you okay? There's not much I can do alone. Please just give me a second to think of a solution," I said to him as he let out soft cries. "I'm sorry, George. I feel bad. I know you're hungry." I scooped him into my arms, and he quieted instantly. I kept him in my arms as we walked around, searching for food before the last light disappeared.

"I'm sorry I got frustrated with you," I said to George. His eyes were so glossy, and I just wanted to give him all the food he wanted. We continued searching for food, as by now, my stomach was rumbling for food, ready to devour enough food for three meals.

As George and I were looking at all of the bushes for fruit, our heads turned when we heard a squealing noise. It was coming from the direction of the village. *Oh no, did something happen? Is someone hurt? Wait, is it a human or an animal? Was it Marcus?* So many thoughts flooded my mind, and I began to panic over the uncertainty of what was happening. *Should I stay here, hide until it stopped, or should I run toward it?*

I was hesitant to walk in that direction. I didn't want to put myself or George in danger. But I was worried that Marcus was hurt or trying to fight off an animal. I swallowed my fear and forced myself forward, step by step, toward the awful sounds ahead.

I quickened my pace, desperate to see what was making the noise. As I got closer, the noise got louder. There was what looked to be a ditch ahead.

"Oh, no," I said, looking at the ditch below. George had his arms wrapped around me, and I held onto him tighter than ever. I stopped in my tracks, unsure of what to do next. "What is that?"

Chapter Twenty-Two

Lightning ripped across the sky, painting it in a blinding white light for a fraction of a second. Thunder followed closely behind, crashing so loud it rattled my chest and caused George to jump across my shoulders with a swift squeal. The rain came down harder, making the ground muddy and slippery. I pushed forward anyway, squinting through the sheets of water as I looked down into the ditch below. "What is that?" I asked aloud, noticing something glinting in the moonlight.

I barely had time to steady myself before my foot slipped, sending me sliding down into the mud. I clutched my side as I looked over to George, who was tugging at my face. That's when I looked out in front of me and saw it: another monkey, just like George, trapped in a little rusted metal cage.

It was smaller than George, with soft brown fur and creamy patches on its belly and chin. The monkey's tiny hands clung to the bars of the cage, and just like George, it squealed louder than I ever thought a creature could squeal.

George screeched and launched himself off my shoulder and shot toward the cage. I got up off the mud as I watched him try and comfort his fellow monkey. George used all his little monkey strength to tug and pull at the sides of the cage. The metal was old and rusted and certainly stronger than him. There was no way George was going to free his friend on his own.

I walked over to them and attempted to lend a human-sized hand or two. I picked up the cage and the monkey and tried my hardest to pull open the front latch of the cage. The metal was twisted, stiff, and wedged out of place. No matter how hard I struggled, the stupid thing refused to budge. The trapped monkey screeched, shaking the cage so violently it shook in my hands as panic surged in my chest. I yanked harder, my palms burning from the friction.

"Ugh, come on…" I muttered through gritted teeth. Mud smeared across my knuckles as I continued to fight against the latch. Rain dripped from my hair into my eyes as I worked. "Come on!"

The cage groaned with the pressure, the old metal creaking until finally the latch gave in with a sharp, snapping sound. I pried the door open, pushing it just wide enough for the monkey to pull itself out. It bolted straight toward George the second it broke free.

The two of them crashed into each other, muddy fur sticking together as if they'd been separated for years. Their little hands clutched tight, claws digging into the other's back, their cries overlapping in sharp, relieved tones that sounded almost like laughter.

George immediately began grooming the other monkey, tugging gently at their wet fur and picking away at the bugs and debris that clung to its fur. He moved so quickly, so thoroughly, as if to make sure the smaller monkey was alright.

I stood there in the mud, rain dripping off my chin, staring like the pieces of some puzzle were finally clicking together. This was what George had been after all along. All the screaming, the squealing, the restless energy that never seemed to let up. He'd been crying for help. Begging, in his own way, for someone to free the one he loved. His mate.

That's why he found me in the jungle that day. That's why he wouldn't leave us alone no matter how irritated Marcus got, no matter how frustrated I felt when he screamed for hours. He was searching for someone, anyone to break open the rusted trap that had stolen his mate from him.

This whole time, I thought he was just making noise. But no, he had a purpose. He had love driving him forward, the same way I had been stumbling through the days, clinging to Marcus even when it hurt. George never gave up, not until his mate was safe in his arms again.

I couldn't help but smile, watching George and his mate cling to each other in the rain. Their little bodies were pressed so close it looked like they might never let go again. It was just them together, safe and whole.

I looked down and noticed George gnawing on something. His tiny hands clutching something tight like it was a treasure. At first, I thought it was just a stick or root he'd dug out of the dirt, but the way the lightning flashed across the object made my breath catch. Gold. A little golden object, half-hidden behind his sharp teeth. My eyes narrowed as I realized what it really was: Marcus's golden compass.

The realization hit me like a crack of thunder from above. Marcus must have slipped his compass into my pocket before I had stormed off. I didn't notice at the time, too focused on my anger and the sting of his betrayal. He was worried about me finding my way back and that he was willing to risk his own safety, even though I had told him I wanted nothing to do with him again.

Marcus didn't have it anymore. Without the compass, he was stumbling blind through this nightmare of endless green walls and twisting roots. I left him with nothing. He was alone. "Oh, no…"

A lump built in my throat as I thought about where he might be now. What if he was in trouble right now? What if he was hurt, or lost, or worse? All because I let my pride drag me away… My anger had burned so hot that I hadn't stopped to think about the cost of leaving him behind in the jungle.

I grabbed the compass from George and clenched the cold metal in my palm. I didn't want to admit it, but I had no choice. I needed to go back and find him. Marcus needed me. And maybe, just maybe, I needed him too.

I turned my head toward the direction of the village, my thoughts tangled into a knot of choices. The pull in my chest to go back for Marcus weighed heavily, but another part of me screamed that if I lost more time, I might never make it back in time to catch the plane home. I stayed still, straining my eyes, when a faint glow flickered in the distance.

At first, I thought my mind was playing tricks on me, conjuring fireflies or reflections in the undergrowth. But the light was steady, moving slowly between the trees and branches. My breath caught.

"Hello?" I called, "Is anyone out there?" The sound echoed through the trees, swallowed by the vastness of the jungle.

A moment passed, long enough for doubt to sink deep into my mind. Then, clear and startling, came a reply. "Hello! Who's out there?"

The words set my heart pounding faster than ever before. Whoever it was, they weren't far. I heard the crunch and snap of twigs nearby, the swish of leaves brushed aside, footsteps pushing closer through the dark. The faint yellow light grew closer by the second.

A moment later, out of the shifting shadows came Savenaca. The lantern in his hand cast a warm ring of light across the damp ground and up the trunks of the nearby trees. The sight of him made my heart sink. I'd been found. "Savenaca!"

"Noah?" Savenaca lifted the lantern higher, the light spilling across his face. "The village has been worried sick," he said, "Everyone thought you were lost at sea. Word had already started to spread that you weren't coming back."

The words hit me harder than I'd expected. I pictured the villagers gathered by the shore, scanning the horizon for any sign of us, probably whispering to one another in anxious tones. Their faith fading with each passing day. Guilt settled like a stone in my stomach. "Savenaca, we need to find Marcus! He's still out there!"

"Come with me," Savenaca said, shifting the lantern so its glow pointed toward the village through the trees. His stance was almost commanding, as though he wasn't giving me a choice in the matter. "We need to get you back to the village."

I shook my head before I even realized I was doing it. "I can't. Marcus is out there, alone and probably afraid! I left him alone, and I have to go back for him." The words came tumbling out, but the urgency inside me was blaring.

Savenaca's brows drew together, "Noah, it's too dangerous. Look around you, the storm hasn't let up. The jungle is flooded with rain and wind. Going back now could cost you your life."

I glanced past him, toward the village. He could lead me home. But my feet refused to move in that direction. My chest tightened with the thought of Marcus wandering alone in the dark. He had no compass, no protection, nothing but himself. I couldn't shake the image of him stumbling, calling out for help, and no one answering.

"I don't care," I said, my voice low but steady. "I have to find him!"

Before Savenaca could reply, I turned back toward the dense stretch of jungle I had come from. The lantern's glow dimmed behind me with each step, swallowed by the darkness until I could only hear the faint sounds of Savenaca calling after me.

"Watch after my monkey for me until I make it back to the village!" I called out to him.

Chapter Twenty-Three

"Marcus?" I called, my voice tearing through the storm. The rain continued to pour down in thick sheets, followed closely by the rolling thunder. It must have been an hour I'd turned back, going further into the depths of the jungle. My throat burned from shouting and calling for Marcus, but still, I kept trying. I had to try.

The sky split in two from another flash of lightning, illuminating the jungle for a blinding moment of light. The branches and leaves glistened in the light, soaking through from the pouring rain. My clothing still clung to me, which, combined with the fact I may have lost Marcus forever, made every step forward feel like I was dragging weights behind me. But nonetheless, I pushed forward.

"Marcus?!" I shouted again, my voice raw. "Marcus, where are you?"

Water streamed down my face, filling my eyes until it was nearly impossible to see past a few steps ahead. The rain was relentless, blurring everything in my vision into abstract shapes and colors. I often found myself stumbling over roots or caught against stray branches, making the journey so much harder than it already was.

The longer I walked, the heavier the thought pressed against my chest. Every second I wasted looking for Marcus and not finding him meant we were farther away from the village. Farther away from my ticket home. The villagers were somewhere behind me, their warmth and certainty lost to the night, lost to the jungle. And here I was pushing further into the nothingness of the jungle.

As I trudged through the rain, I couldn't stop thinking about the compass. Marcus had left me with the key to finding our way back to the village, and I stormed off like his life didn't matter. He had lied to me and he had tricked me, but none of that was worth his life. And now I had his lifeline and he had nothing. If he was lost out here without it, the chances of finding him were getting slimmer by the second.

I cupped my hands around my mouth and screamed again, "Marcus? MARCUS!" The sound cracking in my throat. But the only answer was the endless roar of rain and the crack of branches in the wind. "Please…"

Another hour dragged past, the thought of turning back gnawed at me. My body ached, every muscle was beyond stiff from pushing against the storm, my throat shredded from calling Marcus's name into the jungle. I couldn't tell if I was still moving in the right direction anymore, or if the rain had spun me in circles. For all I knew, I could be walking deeper into nowhere.

Finally, I couldn't force my legs another step. I stumbled into a small clearing, my breath ragged. I decided to take a moment to catch my breath and dropped onto a stump slick with rain. My hands hung limp at my sides, my fingers trembling from exhaustion. I sat there for a few minutes, staring at the ground for a while, watching as the mud puddles broke off into rivers of dirty water racing downhill.

When I finally lifted my head, I realized the clearing opened to a view I hadn't noticed before. Just ahead, beyond the curtain of rain, stretched a small lake. The water's surface rippled and churned under the downpour, every lightning strike casting it in sharp white light before the darkness swallowed it again. The lake looked like an endless sheet of glass breaking apart under the weight of the storm. It was almost mesmerizing.

"Marcus? Please be out here somewhere…" My voice cracked when I whispered Marcus's name again. "Please."

After a moment, the clouds finally shifted just enough for the moon to press through over the lake. Pale light spilled over the clearing, silver streaks running across the lake and painting the water with an almost ghostly glow. Out against the water's edge I could have sworn I saw something. Someone. The silhouette of a person sitting there. I blinked, rubbed at my eyes, and leaned forward on the stump, not sure if the shape I thought I saw was just another trick of exhaustion.

Suddenly, the person moved. My chest tightened and I forced myself to stand, legs trembling as though they'd forgotten how to hold my weight. I squinted through the haze of moonlight and rain, my heart beating so loud I could barely hear the rustle of the leaves around me. The figure shifted again, faint and half-obscured, and I felt my throat close. "Marcus…?"

It wasn't just anyone. The shape of the shoulders, the slouch in the posture—even from a distance—it was unmistakable. The white fabric clung to his frame, soaked through and clinging to his skin. A dirty, rain-darkened white beater. My breath hitched before the words even formed in my head.

It was Marcus.

I recognized him instantly, sitting there at the edge of the water like he'd been pulled straight from a dream. Or a nightmare. My stomach flipped, the heat rushing to my face even though the air was cold and wet. For the last few hours I had pictured him lost, maybe worse, swallowed by the jungle, the storm, or some other danger. And now here he was, lit by the trembling light of the moon.

I slid down the slick mud of the clearing, my hands grabbing at roots and branches to keep from tumbling all the way down. The slope carried me further down toward the water. Splashes of mud and rain mixing together under my shoes. By the time I reached the bank's edge, my legs were coated and my palms stung from clutching at the ground, but none of that mattered. All that mattered was that I'd found him.

Marcus sat there against the water, arms wrapped tightly around his knees so he could hold himself close. His shoulders shook, the motion ragged and uneven. The rain poured down so heavy it should've hidden everything, but I could still see the shine of wetness streaking down his face that wasn't just from the storm. His chest heaved with every breath, quick and shallow.

I started walking up to him, my shoes sinking into the bank. The wet sand almost gave in beneath me, soft and unsteady, but I kept moving closer. His head was bowed, his chin pressed into his knees, his hair plastered dark against his forehead. The sound of him sniffling cut through the patter of the rain.

I froze a few feet from him, watching as the water lapped softly at the bank's edge, Marcus's athletic frame outlined against it. Even hunched in on himself, I could see the tremble in his arms, the way he shivered as though the rain was leeching the last of his strength from him. "Marcus, what are you doing here? We've got to go!"

"We gotta get back to the village," I said, my voice loud to cut through the roar of the rain, "We don't have much time."

"I'm not going back, Noah." Marcus flinched but didn't look up at me. His knees pulled closer to his chest, and his forehead pressed tighter against them. "Just go away," he muttered, "I'm bad and you shouldn't be around me. I lied to you."

He dragged his arm roughly across his face, smearing rain and tears together. His shoulders still hitched, and I could hear the thickness of his breathing even over the storm. His whole body looked small now, nothing like the Marcus I'd gotten used to. "Yeah, I know. I'm not completely over it. But Marcus, the thing is—"

"You said yourself you want nothing to do with me anymore," he interrupted, finally lifting his head just enough that I could see the wet streaks of tears clinging to his cheeks. "I let you down."

The words stung because they were true, but that didn't matter. "You did," I admitted, my voice soft. I took a step closer, mud sucking at my boots. "But you were still looking out for me. You cared about me. That was never part of the lie."

My chest felt heavy saying it, the weight of all the hurt and betrayal mixed with the undeniable fact that even when Marcus screwed up, it was because he thought he was protecting me. He was only trying to do the right thing. The storm cracked above us again, and for a second, everything froze. Everything stood still: the water, the trees, and Marcus hunched and trembling in the rain.

I lowered myself beside him, the mud soaking through my pants in an instant. It was cold and slick against my skin. But I didn't care. Marcus was shaking so hard I could feel it just sitting this close. I reached out and put an arm around his shoulder, pulling him in despite the way his body stiffened at my touch.

"You lied to me because you didn't know what else to do," I said, my voice uneven, fighting the lump in my throat. "And even though that doesn't make it right, I know you only did it because you were scared."

Marcus shifted under my arm, his weight leaning forward. His breath caught, sharp and shaky, and he rubbed at his face again, though it didn't help much with the flood of rain and tears mixing together.

"And I got scared, too," I admitted, my own words heavy, like stones pressing against my ribs. "Because I thought another person I cared about was trying to deceive me for their own terrible reasons." My stomach twisted at the confession, the memory of old wounds brought back into the present.

"I shouldn't have deceived you, Noah," Marcus said, finally turning his head enough that I could see the sadness in his face. His lips trembled as he spoke. "It was selfish."

"Yeah, it was," I said without sugarcoating it, tightening my arm around him so he couldn't shake away from me anymore. "But you know what wasn't selfish? Carrying me after I got sick, finding me food when I couldn't bear the walk anymore, making me a quality breakfast in the middle of freaking nowhere!"

Marcus finally lifted his head, his eyes locking with mine. They were red and raw, but there was something underneath all that pain, like he was waiting for me to pull away. Waiting for me to say the words that would confirm his worst fears. I held his gaze, even though my chest was tight and every beat of my heart felt like it was thudding up into my throat.

"You did all those things because you cared about me," I said, letting the words come out slowly so he couldn't brush them aside. "You didn't lie to me because you didn't trust me. You lied because you were scared I'd hurt you, scared I'd walk away."

"Noah…" His lip trembled, and his arms curled tighter around his knees. I reached down and took his hands gently, peeling them away from his legs. His fingers were trembling, slick from the rain, but I didn't let go. Instead, I pressed his golden compass into his palms and closed his hands around it, holding them there in place.

"You were scared you'd lose me," I whispered, feeling the weight of the compass between us. "But you wouldn't have lost me, Marcus. I'm here for you. I love you."

The storm seemed to ease at that, the pounding sheets of rain breaking apart until only a soft mist lingered in the air. The moonlight pushed through the parting clouds, illuminating the night before us. Marcus shifted beside me, and I caught the sound of his uneven breath. His shoulders trembled before he managed to pull himself together. He met my eyes, and in the pale light his face looks raw, stripped of every wall he'd tried so hard to build.

He sniffled once more, pulling his hands away from mine and letting them sit in his lap. Then, without warning, he leans in and pulls me into him, arms wrapping tight around me as if letting go might send me vanishing into the night. My cheek pressed against his damp shoulder, and I could feel the weight of everything he's carried pressing into me through that grip. My arms slip around his back, holding him there, steadying him in a way I've been aching to since I'd left him.

We sit there like that for a while in silence. The ground beneath us still damp, cold against our legs, but I don't care. The only thing that mattered was the warmth between us, the closeness of his body pressed against mine, the quiet rhythm of his heartbeat I can just barely hear if I focus. The water's edge shimmers faintly in the moonlight a few feet away. It was just me and Marcus again. No lies, no fear, no storm, just us, together in the open night.

"I love you, too."

Chapter Twenty-Four

Marcus cried so hard that my guilt outweighed the shock of his confession.

"I'm sorry, Noah," he said, while tears ran down his face. "I just wanted to be honest with you."

I couldn't think of what to say.

"I felt that I had to lie to make myself seem like half as good a person as you, Noah," he said to me. I didn't think he thought of me so highly. "I didn't realize how much I wanted you until you left me, stranded and alone, trying to find my way back to the village.

I decided that I couldn't stay mad at Marcus any longer. He told me the truth, and I should be happy that he did. I would rather him be honest instead of lying to me.

"Let's walk back to the village together," I said to Marcus.

“You sure?” he asked. “You’re not mad at me anymore?”

“Yes, I’m sure.”

Together, we started the final leg of our journey back. Being with Marcus felt right—like everything had finally fallen into place.

— — — — — — — —

Marcus and I made it back to the village just as the sun had risen over the water. We approached the area where our hut was, and people were giving us looks as if we were a couple because of how close we were standing to each other.

“I think my plane leaves in about an hour,” I said to Marcus.

“Oh,” Marcus said in a depressed tone.

Pretty quickly after people spotted us, a circle formed around us.

“We didn’t think we’d see either of you again,” a lady said before someone else chimed in and added, “We are so glad to see you again.”

“We’re back,” I responded.

“Better than ever,” Marcus said as he glanced over at me.

“We all thought you drowned in the ocean. We were terrified,” a familiar man's voice added. I turned to see Victor standing there with a smile on his face. I hadn't seen him in so long. There were far too many moments where I thought I'd never see him again.

"Are you two okay? Do you need anything? Have you eaten?" Victor kept asking. It felt nice knowing that there are people who care about our wellbeing.

"We found some food along the way," Marcus said. "And had plenty of water."

"Do you need to see the doctor?" Victor asked.

"I think we're good," I replied.

Once everyone's excitement calmed down, most everyone returned back to their respective places and went on with their day. As many left, they gave us hugs and told us how much the village was worried about us.

Victor stayed with us and said to me, "I'm sure you really want to leave here now, huh?" he asked.

"Um…I suppose I do," I responded. I didn't know what to say because while I really wanted to leave, I thought about Marcus and couldn't decide whether it would be worth it to stay for him or not.

"Well, the plane is loaded up and your things are on it. There's a seat for you."

"Okay, cool."

"I forgot one bag in your hut. Let me grab it very quickly."

Marcus and I stood alone together, both unsure what to say.

"It's been a very crazy adventure. I'm really going to miss…you," I said with a stutter, unsure what Marcus would say to that.

"It really has, and I will, too," he said.

Marcus looked like he was trying to hug me, but he stopped. Instead, he reached out his hand, which I slowly lifted mine up, wishing for a hug and not a handshake.

"Come here, silly," Marcus said, pulling me into his arms. We stayed in each other's arms for so long that I lost track of everything going on. Marcus kissed my forehead, and I could hear a sniffle from his nose, so I assumed he was tearing up a bit.

I had to prevent myself from crying, too. I never wanted to leave his arms, but something in me kept telling me I might be better off back in California.

Slowly, we peeled ourselves from each other, and locked eyes with each other for some time.

"I wish you all the best in everything you do, Teachy," Marcus said while trying to conceal his tears.

Hearing this made me want to break down and rethink my decision. But, I didn't know how to react, so I said, "Thank you. I hope you enjoy it here, Preachy," I said with a small laugh.

As I started shuffling toward the plane, I still couldn't take my eyes off of Marcus. *Would I ever see him again? Is he going to stop me?*

Marcus didn't move; he stayed where he was in the sand. Part of me started to feel like Marcus should stop me and keep me here with him, but another part of me thought that I might have to do what my heart is telling me to do, even though I was unsure what that was now.

I watched as tears began to roll down Marcus's face much more, and my eyes welled up. Marcus smiled, as he saw me watch him wipe them off his face like they were not there to begin with.

I started walking up the steps of the plane, and Savenaca was standing next to the steps with the bag that Victor went to get from Marcus's and my hut.

"It's been fun, Savenaca. I'll miss everyone here," I said.

"Bye, Noah. We will miss you, too, but don't forget about Marcus coming with you," she said.

"Marcus? He's not coming with me. I think he wants to stay here, and he didn't mention anything serious about coming back with me to California. He has everything he needs here. He has all of you."

"But he won't have you."

"I don't know. I see it both ways. I didn't have the best luck here, so far. I'm not sure if it will ever get better. For the first time in my life, I felt completely alone. But now, I don't think I've ever felt more found. And it's because of him."

We looked over at Marcus, and he was still watching me from the beach.

"So, don't leave. Why would you leave?"

I thought about it for a moment. I couldn't stop thinking about how Marcus was someone I grew to admire. He did so much for me. Nobody has ever done that for me before.

"I can't," I said to her.

"Can't what?" she asked.

"I can't leave him here. I'm not leaving."

With no doubt, I ran down the stairs, toward Marcus, and we both leaped into each other's arms like nothing could've kept us apart. We hugged each other, and this time I felt like I was at home.

I heard Savenaca say, "Awww."

We looked into each other's eyes after our hug, and we smiled and knew that we were better together.

"Marcus, I–I don't know what to say! Everything I missed back home- the structure, the comfort, the family- I have it all right here with you. I- I love you, Marcus!" I said, hoping he felt the same.

Marcus pulled me in for a kiss, and this kiss felt more romantic than every one we'd shared before. It felt romantic. It wasn't forced. It felt like we both came to terms with the fact that we want each other.

"I love you too, Noah!" Marcus yelled, not afraid of anyone to hear him.

Chapter Twenty-Five

After the finale of our treacherous journey yesterday, it was nice to have a moment—just me and Marcus—together again in the safety of our bure. Our small island home didn't feel so much like a prison anymore. What I once saw as small, empty, and depressing, was now the coziest place I could ask for. It was certainly no hollowed out tree trunk in the middle of the jungle, but we made do.

The sun shined in through the window, casting the two of us a beautiful orange hue. Through the open window, a gentle breeze blew past us—the salty smell of the air that once haunted me now bringing me pure serenity. Outside, the sounds of waves crashing along the shore mixed with the cries of seagulls overhead, made for a perfect day.

I sat in my bed, reading one of the few books I'd brought with me to the island: *It Ends With Us*. It was a book that a friend had recommended to me before I left California. Since I started reading it, I couldn't put it down. In some ways, it reminded me of my own journey on the island with Marcus.

As I turned each page, Marcus had his arm around me, playing with my hair. I would stop reading every few pages, and we would share a few kisses. Marcus would distract me with constant kisses to shift my attention from the book to him. We'd laugh and kiss each other more. When he wasn't kissing me, Marcus just laid there next to me, watching me exist with that big, cheeky grin on his face. I was truly in love with him.

After I finished reading a few chapters, I closed the book and put it on the table next to the window. After I returned to bed, Marcus pulled me closer, looked me in the eyes, and said, "Your body looks so beautiful right now."

"Yeah?" I replied.

"It really does," Marcus said before taking my hand that was lying on the bed and putting it on his chest.

"You look pretty good right now, too," I said, sliding my hand down to his lower abdomen. "I think you should let me show you how beautiful you look right now." I slid my hand down and rubbed it over the fly of his pants, feeling him harden with every passing second.

The lovemaking that followed was more passionate and fulfilling than I'd ever had before. We explored each other in so many positions I'd never tried before. It was bliss, every second of it.

The two of us laid there for the next hour or so, just enjoying being in each other's arms. As much as I enjoyed having relations with Marcus, I think my absolute favorite part of being with him was the cuddles that always followed. He was so tender, so strong. He always knew how to make me feel safe without having to actually do anything. "You're lucky I love you."

"I'm the lucky one," I told him.

After another couple of minutes snuggling in silence, Marcus spoke up again. "Hey, Noah?"

"Yes?" I asked, nuzzling up against his chest.

"Are you sure you made the right choice?" he said, sounding so fragile, "About not taking the plane home? About… me?"

"I'm sure." I said, moving myself up from his chest and planted a very long, very passionate kiss on his lips. "I'm positive I made the right choice, Marcus. I am exactly where I need to be: with you."

Chapter Twenty-Six

Today marked a week since Marcus and I found our way back to the village. A week since the saltwater burned our eyes and our legs nearly gave out beneath the weight of the current. A week since I thought we might never see land again. George stayed close with us, not wanting to leave. The entire village came together to build George a space of his own, so he would never have to be far from Marcus and me. They built a mini replica of our hut for him. Some of my fellow teachers came together and painted George a name plaque to hand outside of his hut. It said: George's Place.

The weather was fairly sunny today. The tide was low, and the beach was filled with seashells. I woke up and found myself cuddled with Marcus's arms around me in bed. I shuffled a bit, just enough to stretch my arms, waking him up. "Good morning," he whispered into my ear.

"Good morning," I replied with a smile.

I have a question for you?" he said softly

"What is it?" I replied.

"Will you be my boyfriend?"

I turned so our eyes could meet, and without hesitation, I replied, "Yes, Marcus. Of course!"

"Teachy is my boyfriend," he said while kissing my neck.

"Only if you will be my boyfriend," I added.

"I will happily be your boyfriend," he said, pulling me closer to him. His bare chest felt so comforting. His skin was so soft, and I couldn't help but stroke my hands all over my boyfriend.

I lay with him, glancing around at our newly updated hut. We had more room now, since Marcus and I decided to share one larger bed instead of two smaller beds. People from all around the village decorated the hut with colorful hand-woven baskets, flowers, and tons of fresh fruit to pick at throughout the day. We were missed, and it warmed my heart to see everyone collectively show their appreciation for us.

"Babe, I have a question for you," Marcus said looking down at me.

I looked over at him and replied, "What is it?"

"Have you told your family that you'll be staying here longer than you originally planned?"

"Yeah, I wrote my mom a note and explained it to her. I have it right here. Can I read it to you and tell me what you think?"

"Yeah," Marcus said, sitting up while I reached for the folded note on the end table.

"Here's what I've got so far:

Dear Mom,

Sorry I haven't written to you sooner! Things have been kinda crazy here. But I do have something to tell you. I have a boyfriend! His name is Marcus. He is so sweet, and you would like him. I am going to stay here a little bit longer than I thought. Things are going well right now. I will update you soon! I miss you!

Love,

Noah

What do you think?" I asked Marcus after I finished reading it to him.

"I think it's great. You must really like me if you're telling your mom about me already," he said while smiling.

"Of course I do," I responded. "I meant to ask you sooner, but what was in the letter that Victor had given you a while back?"

"It wasn't anything important. What's important now is you and I," he said, squeezing me close.

"Guess what else?" I asked Marcus.

"What's that?" Marcus asked.

"I love you," I said before going back to sleep for a bit longer.

"I love you more," Marcus's voice filled the room, reminding me that I was exactly where I should be. I was with Marcus. I was home.

Victor's Letter

Dear Marcus Voss,

I've been trying to find the right words for this, but there's no easy way to say it: I know you're not who you said you were. You're not a missionary, and you never were. I've seen the reports, the inconsistencies, the small details that didn't add up and now, the truth is clear: You lied to us.

Because of this, you no longer have a place here in Taveuni and will be required to leave the island at the end of the week. This is not a request. Whatever mission you thought you were on out here, it's over.

You've done enough damage trying to prove yourself. There's no reason for you to stay any longer.

But before you start packing, there's something else I need you to know, something that's been gnawing at me. I've seen the way you look at Noah. I've seen the way he looks back at you. You can tell yourself it's just friendship, shared hardship, teamwork, whatever you want – but you and I both know it's more than that. It's in the way your voices change around each other, the way you can't stay angry even when you should, the way you two made the best of the stressful situation you were in when you were crammed together in your bure.

As you likely know, Noah Ellison has become homesick and will be returning home soon. He will be returning on the flight at the end of this week as well. Truthfully, we need a missionary here in the village, or at least someone who is strong, noble, and wise like a missionary. You check all those boxes, Marcus, and I would love to keep you here with us. But I think you should go with him.

I know what I said – that you have to return home, but "home" isn't where we send you. Maybe it's where you end up finding the person who keeps you steady when everything else falls apart.

You and Noah belong together. I can see that now, even if you can't yet. Good luck in your future, wherever you end up.

Thank you,

Victor Evans

Victor Evans
Superintendent
Taveuni Learning Academy

About the Author

Eugene Miller

Eugene Miller is an author, educator, entrepreneur, and student from Pittsburgh, Pennsylvania. He launched his self-publishing career at the age of twenty with *The Vampire on Church Street* before later releasing *This House Remembers Every Grief.* He is currently finishing an M.A. in English at Portland State University and lives in Portland, Oregon, where he enjoys reading, writing, traveling, and attending Seattle Mariners games. As a writer, Eugene is especially drawn to experimenting with genre, form, and convention. For more information, visit www.eugenemiller.com.

About The Author

John Reinke

John Reinke is an emerging author and psychology student at the University of Wisconsin-Green Bay. He is passionate about exploring the complexities of human behavior, relationships, and identity, and he weaves these insights into his writing to connect with readers on a personal level. John, a Green Bay native, also enjoys traveling to new places, immersing himself in books, spending time with friends, and advocating for student success. John aims to understand people more deeply and share those reflections in ways that are engaging, thought-provoking, and meaningful to all.

www.ingramcontent.com/pod-product-compliance
Lightning Source LLC
LaVergne TN
LVHW090513110826
845146LV00003B/834